FLAT OUT

Colin Dryden

Colin Dryden

The author, Colin Dryden, knows the motor racing scene well, having covered grand prix racing for nearly 20 years as the staff motor sport correspondent of The Daily Telegraph. He wrote the lives of Jim Clark, Graham Hill and Colin Chapman for the Dictionary of National Biography, and contributes to books and magazines.

He and his wife, Suzanne Hinton, commute between a flat in the City of London and a thatched cottage in Devon where they keep their hot air balloon G-Susi.

After making parachute jumps and then flying hang gliders, Colin Dryden took up ballooning in 1985 in the hope of staying airborne a little longer.

FLAT OUT

Colin Dryden

BUZZARD

First published in Great Britain in 1996 by
BUZZARD BOOKS
PO Box 12493, London EC2Y 8JB

Text © Colin Dryden 1996

Cover by Graham Turner

British Library Cataloguing-in-Publication Data. A catalogue
record for this book is available from the British Library

ISBN 0 9529390 0 2

Printed and bound in Great Britain by
Cox & Wyman Ltd, Reading, Berkshire

For Neil, who loved motor racing

Acknowledgements

FLAT OUT is, of course, a work of fiction, set in an unspecified season in the early 1980s. A problem facing any author writing a novel with a Formula One background is how to give it an air of reality without mentioning actual people, teams and the places where the action takes place.

I am indebted to those All Time Greats of grand prix racing, Sir Jack Brabham, Jackie Stewart and Stirling Moss, as well as Max Mosley, President of the Fédération Internationale de l'Automobile and Professor Sid Watkins, the FIA's Chief Medical Officer; also to the Brabham, Ferrari, Lotus, McLaren and Tyrrell Formula One teams past and present, the Ford Motor Company and the Régie Nationale des Usines Renault SA.

I am also grateful to the following friends and colleagues who either allowed me to include them in the action or gave assistance: Randall Barnett, David Benson, Eric and Ruth Dymock, John Evans, Tony Howard, Patrick Mennem, Richard Murray, John Rawlings, Arthur Reed, Simon Taylor, Graham Turner for designing the cover, Michael Turner and Murray Walker. Above all, to my wife Suzanne.

Will anyone whose name or organisation has been taken in vain please accept my apologies.

*'Bastyan the Bastard' they called Britain's leading
racing driver.*

*Alex Bastyan made too many enemies on his way
to the top but did any hate him enough
to try to kill him?*

DRIVERS WORLD CHAMPIONSHIP	S.AFRICA	LONG BEACH	MONACO	SAN MARINO	BELGIUM	BRITAIN	FRANCE	GERMANY	SPAIN	HOLLAND	AUSTRIA	ITALY	CANADA	BRAZIL	JAPAN	TOTAL
GIANNI ABATI (Ita) *McColl-Renault*	9	9														18
ERWIN SCHRAMMER (WGer) *McColl-Renault*																
JUAN BALTIERI (Arg) *Brabham-Ford*		4														4
WIM HEEMSKERK (NL) *Brabham-Ford*		2														2
GUY ANTONIAZZI (Ita) *Ferrari V-12*	4															4
DINO MORANDINI (Ita) *Ferrari V-12*	3															3
ALEX BASTYAN (GB) *Tremayne-Ford* *(also McColl-Renault)*																
T-N THIBAULT (Fra) *Tremayne-Ford*	1	1														2
HUGO FALCUS (Bel) *Tyrrell-Ford*	6															6
GAVIN BROWN (GB) *Tyrrell-Ford*																
HECTOR BONFANTE (Bra) *McLaren-Ford*		6														6
BENGT CHRISTENSEN (Swe) *McLaren-Ford*																
ALAN MASON (GB) *Lotus-Ford*	2															2
PEDRO JALAPENO (Bra) *Lotus-Ford*		3														3
HARALD KASTNER (WGer) *Fantino-Mostyn*																
TOSHIRO WATANABE (Jpn) *Fantino-Mostyn*																
PATRICK BELLAMOUR (Fra) *Mistral-Ford*																
ROLAND JONCHERY (Fra) *Mistral-Ford*																

1

Alex Bastyan, grand prix racing driver, raised himself on one elbow and let his gaze wander over his team owner's wife, who was lying naked beside him in the best suite of the Hôtel Hermitage, Monte Carlo.

She was a beautiful woman, dark haired, slim, full-breasted. They had just made love and he could see their coalesced sweat glistening on her skin. Caroline Tremayne's eyes were closed and she was breathing deeply as the waves of her pleasure gradually ebbed away.

Alex was suddenly aware of the places where her nails had raked his back in the throes of her passion and he wondered vaguely how he was going to explain away the evidence to his wife. Having to scratch Monegasque mosquito bites seemed a bit lame. He would have to work something out. Olivia was nobody's fool.

He glanced across at his Rolex Oyster, because of its heavy bracelet discarded on the bedside table, and sat up suddenly.

"Omigawd! Is that the time? I've gotta go. Your husband could be here any moment."

His moods could change like weather in the mountains.

One minute, watchful and reserved, the next thunderous. But there was also an element of utter self-control, available at the flick of a mental switch, and this helped to make him – on his day – one of the most feared competitors in Formula One.

Some men drove with their hearts, others with their heads. A very few as if God was in the cockpit watching over them. Alex Bastyan just raced with supreme self-confidence in his own ability. Once committed to a course of action he never backed off and only the extremely foolish would ever try to push their luck with him. On or off the track.

As he stood up, Caroline languidly reached out for him, eyes still closed.

"Darling, where are you? What're you doing?"

"Going, my love. That's what."

"Going? Whatever for? We've only just begun."

"I know. But I can't sing to you now."

Alex started rooting around for his dinner clothes, strewn in the general direction of the chair in the corner of the room.

Caroline Tremayne was normally the most placid and pleasant of women but for the two years since the start of the affair with Alex Bastyan her personality had changed. She was wracked with strange new emotions and feelings. Guilt at being with him, anguish when she didn't see him. Sexual passion that blew her mind to the extent that made her sometimes wonder which was worse: living with the illicit secret or having to go without its fruits so much of the time. And now the man who caused it all was leaving. She hated herself for it, but resentment was taking over. How could he just walk out on her when their lovemaking time together was so precious?

But she was damned if he was going to reduce her to ridiculous tears. Caroline got up from the bed and went into the opulent marbled and gold tapped bathroom for one of the hotel's monogrammed bathrobes.

Alex Bastyan continued dressing. This indifference was

hard to bear. She returned, sat on the bed and said calmly: "I'd leave Freddie tomorrow for you..."

Her words seemed to linger awkwardly between them in the air like an auctioneer's offer attracting no bidders. This had never been in the catalogue but was a lot introduced at the last minute. Facetiously, Eric Morecambe's classic riposte "There's no answer to that!" came to him. Not now on the eve of the Monaco Grand Prix.

He should never have been making love to Freddie Tremayne's wife – gorgeous though she undoubtedly was – the night before the race. Or any race. But she was so desirable and Alex, who long ago had ceased to keep a tally of his conquests, had never known a woman like her. But there was a time and a place and now was the moment to attempt to defuse the ticking bomb. After putting on his shoes he stood up.

"Just tell me one thing, Caroline. You and I are the same age near enough. Freddie's my oldest mate but he's almost from a different generation. You must feel that age gap. Why did you marry him? You must've been fighting off the guys your own age – yet you go for someone even I regard sometimes as almost a sort of father figure. Particularly when he's bollocking me over something I shouldn't've done in the car."

"I suppose I've always looked for father figures," she said. "Besides, I've never cared for young men and rich young men are doubly dreadful. Spoilt brats, most of them. You're the only man of my own age I've ever had a relationship with, believe it or not. Why did I marry Freddie? He's 18 years older than me, by the way. I married Freddie because he was the nicest man I'd ever known.

"He was the first man who seemed to love me for myself instead of wanting to get into my knickers all the time. I suppose women since time began have fallen into that trap. To escape the wolves, you marry the kind old shepherd and then find later that there's more to life than kindness.

"God! What've you done to me? I've always been in control of my life. I'm supposed to be a strong minded woman for heaven's sake. I've helped Freddie build up a team in one of the most competitive areas of world sport – certainly one of the most expensive. We're not one of the big boys like Brabham, McColl, Ferrari or Lotus. But we've had our moments. Runners-up in the constructors' championship – thanks to you. But Freddie built this team. And by God, I've helped him every step of the way.

"But you were only supposed to be our number one driver. A contractual – not a consenting adults in private – arrangement. I don't seem to know what I'm doing half the time. You must forget what I said just now about leaving Freddie. You've addled my wits. I never knew lovemaking could be like it is with you, darling. You've unlocked doors and tapped wellsprings in me I never knew existed."

With his super-fitness and boundless virility, Alex had long ago learned that manners (and iron self-control) maketh man in bed. His previous conquests had been merely physical and he had yet to meet the woman who could outlast him. But with Caroline, the sexual athletics were less important and for the first time in his life he was out of his depth emotionally. So, it seemed, was she. He sought to excuse himself for having started it all.

"It's all my fault - "

"No it isn't. These things always take two people."

"I should never've kissed you like that at that New Year's Eve party at your place. But Freddie's not daft. He must know everyone's lusting after his wife."

"I doubt it. He's in a world of his own. Sponsorship deals, engine deals, contracts for this, and the other, getting new cars designed and built. Just coping with the paper work's enough to drive you potty. I'm only part of the office furniture, not a wife who's suddenly discovered a whole lot of needs and desires. That side of my life has nothing to do with Freddie, I'm afraid. Not that it ever did to any great extent, even before you came into my life."

She shook back her raven hair. "I realise I've got to try and keep my life in two compartments: Freddie and Team Tremayne in one box, and Alex, the love of my life in the other. God! How I hate doing this to Freddie but I just can't help myself."

"What about me? He's the guy who gave me my chance in Formula One, who's stood by me for the best part of a decade. He's my oldest friend and yet I'm – "

"Making love to his wife? Don't you think I feel a million times worse? I *am* the wife. I never thought it was possible to love two men at the same time. But it is. Freddie I love because, well, because he's Freddie. With you, darling, I'm just sort of overwhelmed...." Her voice trailed away.

"You're sure it's not just the sensational sex?"

Caroline blushed. "Of course not. We just seem to meet on every level. I love your mind."

"My mind? You *cannot* be serious. Sportsmen aren't supposed to have minds." He laughed. "Good old Caroline. You can always surprise me. That's the first time anyone's ever said that."

"So you've had lots of women telling you how much they loved you?"

"One or two," he lied. "I'm sorry about all this, ducky. You don't imagine for one second that I enjoy this furtive, wham, bam, thank you, mam, routine, do you? We're here to try to win a motor race. There's no way I should be in your hotel room, late at night, with you starkers - apart from a bathrobe - and me dressed but with guilt written all over me. What on earth could I say if Freddie came in through that door - as he very well might - like something out of a sodding Whitehall farce?"

Caroline laughed for the first time that evening. It reminded him of clear water tinkling over stones in dappled sunlight. How he wished he could make her laugh more often but there was little humour in a fraught adulterous situation, any more than there was in trying to win the Monaco Grand Prix.

"There's a tray in the bathroom," she said, "perhaps we could pass you off as the room service waiter."

"Thanks a bunch. I know we left Freddie getting mildly pissed but I reckon he's still able to tell his number one driver from the Hôtel Hermitage room service – superb though it doubtless is."

"Only joking, darling. You know, I'm getting a bit worried about Freddie. He's drinking more than he used to."

"Probably drowning his sorrows. There's bugger-all for the team to celebrate these days."

Alex drank little, allowing himself the odd glass of champagne. He didn't smoke tobacco or grass, snort cocaine or inject himself with heroin. He was super-fit and bursting with vitality. He was no intellectual, having dropped out after a year reading law at Cambridge and hadn't made a career in the Army. Basically, the only things he was good at were driving and sex. Racing Formula One cars was his work, and as every man needs a hobby, his was chasing girls.

He loved women: the look, the feel, the smell of them. Men were utilitarian creatures designed for hunter-gathering and fighting. Pretty women were fashioned to attract and invite the male to procreate with them. But for the first time in his life he had met his match in Caroline Tremayne.

"You're not listening to a word, Alex." She was talking for the sake of it, determined to keep him in the room with her.

"I sometimes think you're what unites Freddie and me more than anything else. We're both petrified you might leave us. Freddie because he thinks the team couldn't exist without you. After all, Hesketh didn't go on for long after James Hunt went to McLaren in 1976. Poor Freddie. I don't know what he'd do without his fix of Formula One. It's worse than any drug. And I'm – God help me –hooked on you, the man the whole team depends on. What would I do if anything happened to you?"

"Carry on like that and I'll need a larger size in helmets," he said. "But you'd get another driver. We're like number eleven buses. There's always another one along in a minute."

"Don't! I don't mean that. I mean you, the man I love - not the team's number one driver. It's not bloody fair." Caroline sniffed and blew her nose. "There was I swanning along happily enough in my sexual limbo and you turn up like something out of Mills and Boon. I just never knew lovemaking could be like that! It's ridiculous for a woman of my age to be behaving like a sex-crazed teenager. Can you imagine what it's like to slink home to Freddie, all het up, with my pants wet because of you and try to pretend everything's normal?"

Alex sat down beside her on the bed, sneaking a glance at his watch which told him it was nearly 2am.

"Poor old luv. I'd no idea I was causing you all this aggro. We've all got our problems. What's on my mind right now is the race tomorrow. That's what we're here for. Remember what Stirling used to say? Never make love before a long race, only a short one. This one's important so we've already broken Stirling's First Law. And what about Freddie? He could front up any moment. How the hell can the team do its stuff in a few hours' time if the boss has just found his wife being bonked by his number one driver? I should never have come back here with you in the first place. It was sheer madness. I really must go! We've all got to get some sleep, for God's sake."

He stood up and then with a blank expression as if he'd already dismissed her from his thoughts, lifted a great wave of dark hair that had fallen across her face and kissed her forehead.

"Time's up. Byee!" he said.

"Oh God! Don't leave me. Alex. Make love to me all night."

She flung open the bathrobe and lay back, pushing her breasts up at him. Her legs were parted, pubis raised, knees slightly flexed, her whole body in an attitude of supplication. Suddenly she reached up, flung her arms round his neck and tried to pull him down on top of her.

The lure of the full, firm breasts and the great black pubic bush, those hallmarks of her sexuality, was stamped on Alex's senses in a split second. How she knew his weaknesses! He would have to be quick or he would be lost.

Wrenching her arms away, he slapped her face with the palm and then the back of his right hand. They were two light, stinging blows, quick as the flick of a cobra's tongue.

"Let go, you silly bitch. Trying to win the race for you tomorrow outranks fucking you again tonight. Get your priorities right, Caroline. You're the team owner's wife for Christsake!"

* * *

Shutting his ears to her sobs, he strode grim faced down the corridor. Stepping out of the lift in the Hermitage's magnificently absurd rococo foyer, Bastyan nearly bowled over his little team-mate, Teo-Nicolas Thibault, waiting to go up to his own room.

"*Pardon,* Aleex."

"Sorry, Teo!"

Team-mates can be one of Formula One's more ludicrous euphemisms, on a par with 'shunt' instead of terrible accident. In the most competitive sport in the world, the fiercest challenge often comes from the team-mate, particularly if there is a great discrepancy in the pay cheques between an older, more experienced driver and a new number two, with everything to prove.

The younger man's sole aim is to prove that he can out-practice and out-race the old has-been who is unfairly standing in the way, getting the better car and more attention from the race engineers and mechanics. The Tremayne drivers were scarcely on speaking terms, apart from matters directly affecting team strategy, and they were not alone in this.

Team Tremayne had French oil company sponsorship and naturally enough, the company wanted a French driver in the second car and it would have liked one in the first car, too, if possible.

Freddie Tremayne had insisted that Alex was his number one driver and always would be. Thibault, the Tremayne Team second driver, was just over five feet tall. With his initials spelling out TNT, he was inevitably known to the waggish mechanics as Banger Thibault or The Sausage. He had won the Formula Three race at Monaco two years ago, regarded as a good showcase because all the Formula One team managers are there for the next day's grand prix. He went on to clinch the European Formula Three championship and had not been in the least overawed by the move to grand prix driver status. The chauvinistic French press were already tipping him as a world champion one day.

A mass of conflicting emotions: irritation, frustration but anger mainly directed at himself, Bastyan picked his way through all the posers' exotic machinery parked in the Square Beaumarchais, heading for the Hôtel de Paris just round the corner. Team members were spread across the town with the Tremaynes in The Hermitage, Alex Bastyan and his wife Olivia in the Hôtel de Paris and the mechanics in the Holiday Inn.

Freddie Tremayne was to blame for all this. Trying to turn the Monaco race into a social occasion, having their wives there, especially a wife like Caroline. How could he concentrate on the bloody race when the woman who drove him barmy was demanding that he spend all night making love to her?

They should never have got involved but now he, of all people, Mister Use and Abuse'em, was in love? These days he wondered whether he had dropped a match in a firework factory. Much as he needed Caroline, there were times, like just now when he could cheerfully have sent for the fire brigade to cool her down. If only so that he could concentrate on what he was there for – trying to drive her husband's off-the-pace grand prix cars. The team was slipping and everyone knew it. If that wasn't worrying enough, he'd now gone and fallen in love with Tremayne's wife. With all his experience he'd never known such ardour and devotion under such a cool exterior, let alone the sheer naked beauty... Caroline Tremayne was without doubt the most gorgeous woman he had ever known. The combination of poise and passion, intensity and elegance was unnerving. Talk about timing. What a moment to pick. With a grand prix in a few hours' time in an unsorted car and his bloody little team mate Teo-Nicolas Thibault ahead of him on the grid......

There were still plenty of revellers milling around the Casino Square hoping to catch sight of a grand prix driver, film star or other celebrity in town for the race. Many of them seemed to be British, a detachment from one of Page and Moy's jumbo jetloads from Gatwick, doing the rounds of the traditional watering holes, the Tip Top and Rosie's Bar. The better heeled ones might have been dining at Rampoldi's.

One of the more sober fans caught sight of Bastyan and shouted "Go for it Alex!" Others joined in the good natured chorus. He waved with an enthusiasm he didn't feel but it was important to keep up the act. Confidence and aggression, even when the Gatling's jammed and the colonel's dead, were the order of the day. Just then he caught sight of Freddie Tremayne coming down the Casino steps.

In complete contrast to his beautifully turned-out wife, Tremayne was a large, amiable, ill-co-ordinated man who could even look untidy in a dinner jacket. No collar was ever uncurled or pocket without a bulge. His doctor said his high colour was due more to blood pressure than rude health and had proposed a less stressful way of life than Formula One team ownership. Freddie, who could envisage nothing else, carried on as usual, his grey hair getting ever more unruly in its battle with the expensive taming gel that Caroline insisted upon for the more important social occasions.

Exuding bonhomie, whiffs of Remy Martin and an oboe-sized cigar, he ambled over and clapped his driver affectionately on the shoulder.

"Pasht your bedtime isn't it Alex? Important day tomorrow. Thish ish Der Big One. Ther one we've gotta win!"

"You bet, Freddie. But I'd feel one helluva sight happier if we'd got the handling sorted. Street circuits aren't my bag, you know that. I'm a wide open spaces man."

Tremayne swayed slightly and beamed. "Don't worry about a thing, old boy. Get a good night's sleep." He pulled himself together and was completely serious. "Mac and his boys've been toiling away while we've been swanning and I've just had a message to say they reckon they've cracked your handling problem. It was the springs and dampers. A faulty batch apparently. Everything's been changed and they're sure you'll be OK now for the warm-up and the race. I must admit I've had more than I should to celebrate in advance. It'll be all hunky-dory, you'll see."

"Let's hope so," said Alex. "I've always wanted to win here. I'll try to sleep a bit easier now, though."

"You do that. I shan't be far behind you. My lovely wife is waiting for me.... Everything'll be fine tomorrow."

Freddie turned to go and seemingly tired by the effort of concentration, nearly fell over the kerb. Alex grabbed the big man's elbow, the movement making his back tingle with the livid little reminders of Caroline's finger nails.

What a hope! he thought. The boss is pissed as a newt. There's only Mac's guess that the car's sorted. I've been in bed with the boss's wife and then thumped her and he's tight as a tick. Freddie was no lush. What had got into the man? Everyone was letting the side down this Monaco.

But it had been the mention of Caroline that made him wince. However hard he tried to concentrate on steering the right course, she would always be there, just below the surface, like a dolphin keeping station.

2

Team chief speak not with forked tongue, Alex told himself through gritted teeth as his helmeted head snapped back through the fierce acceleration up the hill from St. Devote. He snatched third gear as he streaked past Rosie's Bar, then fourth gear with the exhaust note blatting off the big hotels looking out to sea and even fifth for a split second before braking hard for the turn in to Casino Square.

Whatever Mac and his boys had been doing in the garage while he'd been fornicating in the Hôtel de Paris last night had transformed the handling. He was now in business and must stand as good a chance as anyone in the lottery that was the Monaco Grand Prix.

This was the half hour warm-up or untimed practice session, the last chance saloon for man and car with problems held in the morning before the 3.30pm start. Times out on the circuit did not count for the starting grid which had already been decided in final practice on Saturday afternoon.

Monaco was a law unto itself over practice times, as with so many other things. First practice was on Thursday with a free day on the Friday, which is used for training by other circuits. This was assumed by the cynical British press to be a smart move to get as many people as possible staying an extra day and spending more money in the tiny tax haven. It might have helped offset the infuriating loss of revenue due to so many people being able to see the race for nothing from hotels, houses, flats, cafés and other vantage points over which the Automobile Club de Monaco had no control.

Organisers' problems were the last thing on Alex's mind as he took advantage of a surprisingly empty track to put together a fast lap in a car he scarcely recognised from those frustrating official practice sessions. It now had good traction out of the really slow corners and handled like a dream on the quicker ones. Mac was a sodding genius but why couldn't he have done it earlier?

Race average speeds at Monaco of a little over 80 mph might seem derisory compared with the 150 mph attainable on the wide open spaces of Monza and Spa but the street circuit was always one of the sternest examinations of a driver's skill in the Formula One calendar. The utmost precision was called for over every inch of the two-and-a-bit miles lined with Armco crash barrier like a giant Scalextric set. A mistake in the lead at Silverstone, for example, could lead to a spin on the grass and a chance to rejoin the fray, with the driver shaken but still possibly third. An error at Monaco was invariably final. There were no run-off areas, only an implacable barrier waiting to smash wheels, tear off front wings and crush bodywork as the penalty for the slightest indiscretion.

There was little space for grass, where two tower blocks have to grow when only one grew before. Lack of elbow room had led to land being reclaimed from the sea, more in the interests of leisure than housing. Level playing fields were hard to find in the more hemmed-in coastal towns of the Côte d'Azur.

With no straights worthy of the name, the exit from every bend seemed to lead directly to the turn-in point for the next.

Car handling had to be as neutral as possible and a quick lap calls for near perfection on every corner.

"Well done, Alex!"

Stopwatch in hand, Freddie Tremayne was jubilant when Bastyan pulled into the pits. "Terrific stuff. I reckon your last complete lap would've put you on the second row. And you were on race tyres, not qualifiers. Looks as though we've cracked it!"

"Nothing to do with me," said Alex, peeling off his Nomex balaclava. "Put it down to Mac and his boys getting it right and my getting a clear run for once."

He and Freddie headed off to the motor home for debriefing with Jim MacGregor and his engineers, known to the mechanics as Big Mac and the Burgers. Teo-Nicolas Thibault sat smugly on the pit counter, resigned to his sixth row place on the grid, but happy in the knowledge he was two ahead of his team-mate.

Watch it my little froggy friend, I'll be having your guts for garters, this afternoon, Alex said to himself as they passed.

3

"The race is running true to form!" Mike Morgan bellowed in the ear of his colleague, Peter Randall. They were sitting side by side opposite the pits behind the Armco and 10 ft high debris-fencing on two of the handful of seats allocated to the writing press.

The very nature of their work made journalists gregarious. As any TV wildlife programme viewer knows, it takes more than one jackal to pull down even the smallest young wildebeest on the plains of the Serengeti. Similarly, the Formula One press fraternity soon learned to hunt its prey in packs, subdivided into pairs.

The sheer impossibility of one reporter being able to keep tabs on the 20-odd drivers at a grand prix meeting called for a pooling of resources. "You get a quote from Johnny Abati and I'll have a word with Alan Mason," became the order of the day. Photographers depended on each other even more. The incident that missed the camera's eye was lost forever, although it could be recreated to some extent by a reporter from eyewitness's accounts.

That was why every front page carried exactly the same shot of a spectacular crash. The picture would be taken by the one man who happened to be in the right place at the right time passing on a print under the Old Photographic Pals' Act to his rivals, because that is the only way they could cover miles of track. No man dared welsh on the agreement because he would be ostracised and could then miss out on the big one himself some day.

However cut-throat the competition between newspaper or magazine proprietors, their employees enjoyed a camaraderie, travelling, drinking together, staying in the same hotels and helping each other out professionally. Provided they showed the right attitude, newcomers were welcomed to Formula One coverage, admitted to the pack, advised how to go about things and assigned a minder.

Mike Morgan was a stocky, volatile Welshman, who delighted in telling anyone who cared to listen that he was a Motor Sport Martyr from Merthyr Tydfil. (He came from Swansea but Merthyr was better for the alliteration.) An enthusiast through and through, he claimed a penchant for night rallying had cost him his first marriage while his devotion to international grand prix coverage denied him the chance of re-marriage and the blessings of a happy family life. It also left him free for the good natured pursuit of any fine looking women he met. This was on the basis that all short Welshmen since Lloyd George were expected to be randy, so who was he to let the side down?

An excellent journalist with a neat turn of phrase, his easy going manner made him a popular figure in the pit lane. Mike Morgan was one of the growing band of specialist motor sport magazine writers who also supplied much briefer reports on the day to a Fleet Street tabloid without its own staff Formula One correspondent.

Peter Randall, whom he was looking after, was a pink-cheeked young man of 21 from Grimsby who had escaped the drudgery of weekly newspapers by answering an advertisement for staff on a new motor sport magazine. He was convinced he had landed the job only because no one else would take it at the salary offered. He was in his first season of Formula One coverage and extremely grateful for Morgan's tuition.

Conversation was difficult enough out in the open at a motor race and it is near impossible at Monaco where the roar of 10,000 horsepower is amplified by the architecture. Only as the race progressed, cars dropped out and gaps appeared in the torrent of metal thundering through the streets, was it easier to make yourself heard in the alfresco press box.

"I reckon it's less than half the field still running," Randall shouted, "and four changes of leader."

Morgan consulted his lap chart.

"I make it five. Poor Johnny Abati must've felt he'd got it made until he got that puncture in the tunnel. Let's see who we've got left. Hector Bonfante's going great guns in the McLaren, he's got 20 seconds over Hugo Falcus in the Tyrrell. A pity Antoniazzi and Morandini are out in the Ferraris. I always like to see a red car do well – but not too well. Baltieri's doing OK in the Brabham. But watch Alex Bastyan. He's running strongly in fourth, swarming all over Juan's car. You see he's got past Thibault, much to the little grenouille's chagrin, I fancy boyo."

"Thibault isn't giving up," said Randall. "He's hanging on like sodding limpet."

"There's a lot of needle between those two. I only hope they don't push each other off. Not to put too fine a point on it, they hate each other's guts. Christ! Bonfante's out. That puts Hugo Falcus's Tyrrell in the lead with Baltieri's Brabham second and Alex third in the Tremayne. This is getting *very* interesting. Anything can happen. Do I sniff the possibility of a British win? How many laps to go?

"Nineteen, I make it," said Randall.

"Let's see," said Morgan. "Who've we got? Falcus, Tyrrell; Baltieri, Brabham; Bastyan and Thibault in the two Tremaynes

– Big Mac's done a good job there with both his cars running – young Schrammer in the second McColl; Bengt Christensen, McLaren and Alan Mason in the Lotus. Seven runners left and 19 laps. It's anybody's race. Come on Alex! Let's have a Brit winning for once. Not that we're partisan or biased, boyo."

"Not 'arf," said Randall with a grin. It was all new and wonderful to him and he was enjoying every moment. To be surrounded by all the magic and glamour of Monte Carlo when he might have been writing up his district council reports in his mother's front room, struck him as the height of human happiness. Even if he was being deafened and constantly having to adjust his ear defenders to catch what Morgan was saying. He looked up at the board giving the position of the leaders.

"Jeez! Hugo Falcus is out now. I thought I missed him last time round."

"Judging by that great cloud of steam and smoke over the way, he's retired the Tyrrell in the pits," said Morgan. "This race is a car killer, always has been. That puts Juan Baltieri's Brabham in the lead with Alex second and Thibault third. A great day for Freddie Tremayne for once."

"Baltieri's in trouble," said Randall. "Did you notice how his engine was misfiring as he came by last time?"

"Double trouble," replied Morgan. "He's dinged something and his front wing is being worn at a very rakish angle. That Brabham's got to be a pig to drive now and I fancy we won't see him next time round."

"That'll put Alex in the lead!" said Randall excitedly.

"Precisely! Got it in one, boyo. Here he comes! He's going better than ever." Morgan clicked his stopwatch and again as Thibault in the second blue and green car flashed by.

"Something's happened there. Alex's got 25 seconds over Thibault. We've got Bastyan, Thibault, Schrammer, Christensen, and Mason two laps adrift in the Lotus. Five runners left and five laps to go. At this rate we could have no one running at the finish. What a race! Can you watch them home while I nip over the bridge to the other side for the finish?"

"OK," said Randall nervously.

All eyes were turned to the right as Bastyan's Tremayne-Ford flashed over the line and swivelled to watch it disappear round Ste Devote. He was now lapping like clockwork on the empty track reeling off 1 minute 33 second laps and increasing the gap between himself and Thibault. Erwin Schrammer seemed about to collect his first championship points in the second McColl with Bengt Christensen fourth and Alan Mason was limping round in the Lotus and unlikely to finish.

The last lap. On cue, the Tremayne-Ford could be heard coming out of the tunnel, changing down for the chicane, accelerating through the Tabac corner and the first half of swimming pool complex, slowing for the second half and for the Rascasse and Antony Noghes corners.

Instead of the roar of acceleration as the triumphant driver put down the power for the last time on the finishing straight there was an uncanny silence. All eyes strained to the right. Then the Tremayne-Ford came into sight, slowly coasting to a halt within sight of the chequered flag to a great groan of sympathy from the crowd.

Murray Walker, who had been conveying the drama of the race to television viewers in Britain in his own inimitable fashion, was beside himself with excitement in the commentary box.

"What terrible, frightful luck. Bastyan must've run out of fuel in the last few yards. What a tragedy! He must be absolutely, utterly distraught after his best drive for ages. What a thing to happen to the Tremayne team which deserves a slice of luck. What am I saying? They will have a victory because Teo-Nicolas Thibault, that doughty little Frenchman who's Bastyan's team mate, isn't far behind.

"Wait a minute! The camera's looking for Thibault, waiting for him to come out of the tunnel. Now it's back on Bastyan. This is fantastic! He's out of the car and trying to push it to the line! Can he get it there before his team-mate comes round? It'll be a great incentive because there's no love lost between those two, I can tell you.

"Bastyan looks absolutely shattered. He's flipped up his visor but he must be gasping for air with the effort. He's one of the fittest men in grand prix racing but you need to be, trying to push a car after 75 laps of this circuit. The crowd are roaring him on even though a Frenchman is chasing him. What a tribute to the sportsmanship of this crowd here! They're torn between what to cheer for, sheer British guts or French dash.

"I wonder what instructions Thibault's been given over the radio? Erwin Schrammer's still running in the McColl and so are Bengt Christensen in the McLaren and Alan Mason in the Lotus. I can't imagine the little Frenchman hanging back to let Bastyan win. I may be wrong but I suspect he's driving like a tiger to try to snatch his first victory from his team-mate.

"Bastyan is still pushing. He's got perhaps 100 yards to go. All you can hear is the crowd roaring him on. He's on his knees! He staggered a bit there and slipped but he's up again and pushing. Thibault's just out of the tunnel! He must do it now.

"He must be able to cover that length of track at racing speed on light tanks - let's hope not too light like Bastyan's - in the time it takes Alex to push his car to the line. No! I don't believe it. It's incredible. Thibault has crashed at the swimming pool! He must've got over-excited. Aren't we all? What a stupendous race. There goes Tremaynes' chance of a one-two but it's still all down to Bastyan. Alan Mason's still running but he's two laps behind. But Schrammer's McColl is on the same lap.

"This is the most sen-*sational* finish I've ever seen! I do believe Alex Bastyan is going to do it. Young Schrammer - what a cool head on young shoulders - is not going to make the same mistake as Thibault. I shouldn't say that. But he isn't.

He's rounded the last corner. It's going to be man on foot against 400 horsepower.

"Alex is going to do it. He's done it! He's done it! He's got the Tremayne's nose over the line just as Schrammer's McColl crosses it. What a motor race! *Fan-tastic!* Those must be the hardest earned nine points in grand prix racing. So it's six points to Schrammer, McColl; four to the Swedish driver Bengt Christensen, McLaren, and three for Alan Mason, Lotus, with no other finishers in the most incredible Monaco Grand Prix I've ever seen."

As Murray Walker stopped to draw breath, millions of armchair enthusiasts sighed with relief, pulled the ring on another beer can, sipped their Moët & Chandon or popped out to put the kettle on.

* * *

The last few steps drained what was left of his strength. He slipped and fell on his knees, his red gloved right hand still on the cockpit coaming. Unknowingly, he had crossed the line and the chequered flag swirled about him as if the Automobile Club de Monaco official wanted to wrap up Bastyan as well as the race.

The pit area erupted.

Everyone in the stands opposite was on their feet.

Click! Click! Click!

The photographers' camera shutters rattled away in the uncanny silence. The sound of the two cars still running on other parts of the circuit was merely distant thunder. The British photographers were salivating at the dramatic possibilities. They could already see themselves in dinner jackets at the London Hilton stepping up to receive the Sports Photographer of the Year award.

Marshals further down the short curved finishing straight

frantically waved their yellow flags to warn the oncoming drivers to slow for the stranded driver and car on the finishing line.

Freddie Tremayne and Jim MacGregor exchanged worried glances and, as one man, stepped on to the track. Taking an arm each around their shoulders, they dragged Alex to the pit lane as marshals pushed the car to one side.

Click! Click! Click!

First there had been RACE ACE PUSHES CAR TO VICTORY. But this was even better as the burly forms of team owner and designer flanked the slim overalled figure of Alex Bastyan, helmeted head lolling and feet dragging.

Click! Click! Click!

RACE ACE CARRIED LIKE RAG DOLL. Only feasting piranhas could have matched the snapping frenzy. Each camera was operated as if lives as well as livelihoods depended on it.

Freddie and Jim got Alex to a plastic chair and sat him down.

Click! Click! Click!

RACE ACE KO'd IN CHAIR. Whatever their nationality, what a picture spread for the newspaper staff men! What earnings for the freelances! What a pity some of them were in honour bound to share their golden rolls of film with colleagues who had wrongly gambled on getting more newsworthy shots at the Loewes Hairpin or Casino Square.

Click! Click! Click!

"Get his helmet off."

"Get away! Stand back, you buggers. Give him some air for God's sake." This was an anxious Freddie Tremayne to the ever encroaching lensmen who had formed a circle for the kill.

"It's heat exhaustion. Dehydration. He'll be OK."

"Shall we try and get Sid Watkins to him?"

"Just bring him round. We'll ask the Prof. to check him over later."

Jim had eased off the helmet and unpeeled the sweat-soaked balaclava from a reddened face, lined with effort and exhaustion. Alex looked years older than the man who had started the race. Freddie tried to force the blue plastic neck of a bottle of Evian water between Alex's teeth. Then he poured it over his head and gently slapped his face.

"What's the best way to bring him round?"

"Try telling him he won - see if that gets through?" suggested Jim.

"You won, Alex! You won!" Freddie kept repeating between the waterings.

The grey-green eyes were now half open but glazed and uncomprehending.

Click! Click! Click!

RACE ACE IN COMA? This photo story still had legs and the cameras clicked away as long as there was film to be used.

Freddie still persevered. "You won, Alex. But we didn't get a one-two because the Banger crashed at the swimming pool."

Alex stirred slightly and mumbled something.

Freddie exchanged glances with Jim. "He's coming round. What's that you said, Alex?"

"Shay that again, Freddie. The last bit," Alex murmured.

"He's rambling. What did I say Jim?

"Let me see? Wasn't it that we hadn't got a one-two because the Banger had crashed."

A faint smile spread over Alex's haggard face. He sat up, shook his head and ruffled his hair as if trying to unscramble his brains. Then he reached out, took the bottle from Freddie's hand and glugged greedily on it.

"Sorry you didn't get your one-two for the Constructors, Freddie," he said. "But that little bugger didn't deserve six points. He was up my chuff for half the race trying to pressure me into a mistake. It was sheer poetic justice and the best of frogs' luck. To the victor the spoils! I've got a cup to collect."

Alex got to his feet, zipped up his overalls, tried to wipe the sweat off his face and hands, squared his shoulders and walked as nonchalantly as he could across the track to the red draped royal box. Not for him the swagger affected by some drivers. He waved his Goodyear cap in thanks to the crowds along the straight who had just cheered him as he struggled to the line. They roared back: "Aleex! Aleex!"

A firm handshake from the Prince brought the quaintly light-headed thought that if both of them had been any good at cricket and at the same age they might have met as schoolboys. The match against HSH's school had been one of the highlights of his own summer terms.

A delightful smile from Her Serene Highness and a genuinely concerned inquiry about his health left him feeling charmed and instantly better. If the princesses of the Middle Ages looked like her, it was little wonder the citizenry of the day believed the royal touch could cure anything from the black death to tennis elbow.

There was more applause to be diffidently acknowledged as he walked across the opulent foyer of the Hôtel de Paris, carrying the splendid trophy and his helmet. As always on race days he had withdrawn into his shell like a hermit crab in order to bring every fibre of his being to bear on the afternoon's work. Concentration, exhaustion and elation had later left room for nothing else. Going up in the lift to his hotel room, Alex had a sudden premonition that Olivia somehow knew he had been with Caroline. But he was almost too tired to care that victory on the streets would count for little in the marital scales against adultery between the sheets.

4

As Alex eased himself into the soothing bathwater with a sigh of pleasure, his wife came in, sat on the mahogany lid of the lavatory seat and launched her attack. Olivia was small and slim, not the sort of woman to earn a building worker's wolf whistle. In the early days of the marriage her regular features often wore an air of wistful sadness. Nowadays they were more resolute than resigned, and by the time she was fifty her expression would have the severity of a judge sentencing paedophiles.

"I'm not as daft as I look," she said. "I deliberately refrained from saying anything earlier because I know how you need to concentrate and psych yourself up before a race. But now you've won I'm going to have my say. It doesn't really need a Sherlock Holmes to deduce that something's going on when your husband creeps in at two o'clock in the morning with his back looking like he's been wrestling the Esso tiger. Caroline, I presume, or did you ditch her and pick up some other tart once I was out of the way?"

"Of course it was Caroline. But how – ?"

"Did I know?" Olivia smirked. "You can't hide your back in a room full of mirrors. Besides you reeked of her. Couldn't you even have showered before getting into my bed? I've tried to turn a blind eye to your sordid amours but when they're conducted under my very nose, it's more than even I can take. I know you don't love me. You've never loved me – it was only my father's money. But to go screwing your best friend's wife when I'm here with you is pretty low - even by your standards."

Alex was exhausted. If it wasn't so serious it would almost be comic. He'd just won the race he most wanted to win in his life, something that made him a hero in the eyes of the world. Hundreds of millions of people had seen it on TV and millions more would read about it in their newspapers and magazines. Yet here he was being nagged rotten by the women in his life. The woman he now knew he truly loved had caused a scene last night and now his wife was giving him hell - deservedly - in the post-race bath. The only thing in his favour was that he had won the race and it wasn't an early one.

In a symbolic gesture of resignation and escape he submerged but with protective hands over his genitals, a wall of one, facing the other side's free kick. It was one of life's little ironies that the vital organs that gave man his greatest pleasure not only got him into so much trouble but were so desperately vulnerable.

Olivia sat there unmoved. There was no inspiration to be had under the scented waters. As he surfaced, Alex knew his behaviour was inexcusable and there was no way out.

"I'm sorry, Olivia," he said at last. "Why on earth do you put up with me?"

The direct approach always worked best. Disarm the opponent by conceding her main point. It was a language they both understood. Theirs was no love match but they had stuck it out for a decade now, despite his uncounted infidelities. He knew he was on the right track because she got up, walked over and perched on the edge of the bath, trailing the fingers of her right hand in the frothy green water.

"Good question," she said in a voice that had thawed a few degrees. "Put it down to habit as much as anything. I've always assumed - perhaps foolishly - that whatever you did, you'd always come back to me. But after this weekend's performance I'm beginning to wonder whether I care one way or the other."

Alex could only shrug helplessly. "I guess I deserve that," he said.

"We've always done our own things, had our own space," Olivia went on. "But why do you have to keep rubbing my nose in your dirty doings as if I'm some puppy to be house-trained? I know you've been having affairs for years but please don't conduct them under my very nose. It's so humiliating. I realise you can't really help it and that you're all the time looking for the love I can't give you and that you never had as a child. Just try to be a bit more subtle about it. Is that so much to ask?"

Alex was astonished. They had never had a conversation like this. Olivia seemed to know him better than he knew himself.

"Of course it isn't. I've behaved abominably and I really will try to turn over a new leaf."

"I've heard that one before. You know, I sometimes think our marriage only exists because you and Daddy get on so well. He gave you your start in motor racing and the interest you pay on the loan - all right, I know it was a gift - is to stay married to me."

Alex made as if to interrupt her but the look she gave him made him think twice. She'd not finished with him yet.

"You've made your own way since, I grant you, and you're a far bigger star in your world than I am in mine. But you're still quite happy to live with little old me in the house my father bought us when you hadn't a bean. You go on keeping up the pretence of being married to me. You could move out tomorrow and set up house with one of your women. Why don't you?"

Just when it looked as though the fire was dying down it had flared up again.

"Do you want a divorce, then?" he asked flatly.

"I didn't say that, though God knows I've got grounds. I'm just curious as to why you want to go on with this... this mockery of a marriage."

He didn't know what to do. How could you have a conversation like this when they were due at the Sporting Club gala dinner that evening? Women had no sense of occasion. Like most men and especially those with high-risk, exciting occupations, he liked a quiet life at home. What a pity his lifestyle didn't permit it.

Rising from the water and taking care to cover himself carefully with the towel, he then sat glumly on the edge of the bath and dried his hair. He knew he was betraying Caroline but their time would come later. All he could think of was the need to paper over the cracks in a cowardly fashion.

"I know our marriage isn't the greatest, Olivia. Whose is these days? But we're still together after 10 years. That must count for something, surely? What on earth would Stan and Edna think if we split up? Old Stan'll be tickled pink at my win today. He should've been here but he had some charity golf weekend he couldn't get out of. I can see him now, buying drinks all round at the 19th hole and telling all his cronies how his son-in-law's famous victory is all down to him and what a great talent spotter he is. You hit the nail on the head just now. Habit, you said. We've been civilised up to now so why don't we just go on as we are for a bit, Olivia? Give it our best shot, eh?"

His wife half smiled for the first time that evening.

"You men are all the same. You expect to be able to do what you like but dodge the consequences and still have a quiet life when you get home. But this is your big day and, believe it or not, I am pleased for you. As a wife – even an unwanted one – I do bask in some of the reflected glory, you know. Don't worry. I shan't embarrass you in your hour of triumph. I shall be the dutiful wife at your side at the Sporting Club, keeping up appearances. But that's for the outside world – for general consumption because we're in foreign parts. In return, I want your promise not to go on seeing Caroline."

"It's a deal."

He hated himself as he spoke but buying off trouble was all he could expect for the moment. Olivia looked at him sharply but said nothing and shrugged.

"I'll leave you to get dressed. We can't go on like this, Alex. You and I need to do some serious talking about the future."

5

It had been a weekend of mixed fortunes for the principals of the Tremayne team as they waited in the departure lounge of L'Aéroport Nice Côte d'Azur for the Monday afternoon BA Tristar to London, Heathrow. Freddie was delighted the race had been won but miffed that he had not scored maximum constructors' championship points with first *and* second places. Caroline thought a race had been won but her lover was now lost. She wondered how and when she would see him again. Olivia had monopolised Alex at the dinner last night and now, at the airport, so that she couldn't get near him.

Alex was still on his race winner's high, the euphoria level slightly lowered by Olivia's presence. But God bless her, she had been as good as her word and there had been no scenes at the gala dinner. As soon as they arrived at the airport Olivia had headed straight for the flight's check-in desk and set about organising the seating arrangements. She made sure she had a window seat, with Alex next to her and Freddie Tremayne on his right with Caroline out on a limb the other side of the aisle.

This well suited Alex who was determined to let Freddie know exactly how he felt about Teo-Nicolas Thibault whom they'd left in the airport waiting for an Air Inter flight to Marseilles.

"I'm sorry to keep on about this," he said as soon as they were seated, "and I know you're upset that we didn't get a one-two but we nearly got bugger-all. I don't know if the cameras showed it but the little sod was trying to push me off for the best part of 40 laps. I swear he was trying to pressure me into dropping a bollock so that he could win. Who the hell does he think he is? Don't you give him any team orders, Freddie?"

"Of course I do. But it's not as simple as that. There are political considerations as well."

"What political considerations, for God's sake?"

Freddie lowered his voice. You never knew if a pressman might be sitting nearby.

"He thinks that the sponsorship money he brings to the team - you know how much better the French are at promoting their drivers than we are – entitles him to be numero un, as he puts it."

"I'll give him numero un! The little sod. Our gentleman's agreement says I'm the numero uno. In perpetuity. Till hell freezes over. Till death do us part etcetera, etcetera."

"I'm afraid things have changed a bit since we started out together, Alex. Do you know what he said to me the other day? 'Wizzout ze monnaie I bring to ze Tremayne team wiz my sponsors you would be feenished, Freddie!'"

"He said that, did he? Cheeky little bastard. I hope you sent him away with a kick up the arse."

"I couldn't really. It's truer than he knows, more's the pity. We've always been over-dependent on French sponsorship. I just can't get British companies to invest in us."

"Stupid sods. What's the matter with 'em."

"I'm afraid the people who run them haven't got the vision to see the advantages of having their name on a mobile billboard seen by 400 million people 16 times a year. It's all part of our insularity, I suppose. We can't think further than Wolverhampton. But your win yesterday's done us the power of good. Even if we never win anything again – which God forbid – this Monaco will always be remembered as the race where Alex Bastyan pushed the Tremayne-Ford to victory!"

And I'll also remember it as the weekend where I nearly got divorced, thought Alex. Aloud, he said: "I'm sorry you're having aggro with the sponsorship, Freddie. But that's your problem. Mine is to try to win races, and failing that, to score as many points as poss. It's not made any easier by the Banger. Hasn't he read any of the annuals about previous seasons or does he think it all began when he got his fucking little French *derrière* in the seat of an F1 car?

"Haven't you told him about the '78 season when Mario Andretti was winning everything in sight for Lotus and Ronnie Peterson followed him round like a dog on a lead? Don't you think Ronnie could have passed Mario if he'd wanted to? But he obeyed team orders. Colin Chapman had decided it was going to be Mario's year. It happened. Why? Because Ronnie obeyed team orders.

"And didn't Neubauer call the Mercedes team 'The Train' because Stirling followed in Fangio's wheeltracks? If great drivers - and I mean great - can follow team orders, who is this jumped-up little Gallic git to think he can defy you and try to give me grief? No one should drive when they're seething with rage. You've got to be as clinical as you can and concentrate. That little bugger is getting on my tits, Freddie, and unless you do something about him I can't answer for the consequences."

"Ever done any man management, Alex?" asked Freddie a trifle wearily.

"Only in the army, ages ago. As I recall, the military concept of man management is to bark an order at an inferior rank and put him on a fizzer – that's a charge – if he doesn't obey instantly. Simple. A pity you can't do that."

"If only life were that easy," mused Freddie. "No wonder a lot of service types are all at sea once they're exposed to the harsh conditions of civilian life. You know Alex, Teo-Nicolas is not a bad little chap. We've had worse. He's terribly ambitious and I like that in a driver – the will to win, to succeed at all costs."

"But not at my bloody cost. His job is to ride shotgun to me in this outfit, not take over the sodding reins."

"I know, Alex, I know. I've had words with him and told him to cool it. If he hadn't got over-excited on the last lap we'd've had a one-two yesterday and I've given him a good bollocking. He's promised to reform but I think part of the trouble between you two is that you're such a Francophobe."

"I am not!" Alex was outraged. "I love everything French – apart from my team-mate." With Olivia sitting next to him he could scarcely extol the expertise of French women between the sheets. Ticking each item off on his fingers, he continued: "I love France, the way of life, the countryside, the food. The wine I'm having to save for my retirement, *faute de mieux* – you see, I've even got a bit of the lingo – but I do allow myself a little champagne now and then, as you know. The nation that produces Bollinger as well as the Banger can't be all bad. I salute it," he said with a huge grin.

After the passengers had admired the beauties of the Alps and been told that Mont Blanc was clearly visible on the left hand side, Captain John Evans ended his in-flight information announcement.

"As I'm sure many of you are returning to London from the Monaco Grand Prix yesterday, I'm delighted to say that we have Mr Alex Bastyan, winner of that very exciting race, on board with us this afternoon."

This produced a surprised ripple of applause and a buzz of conversation as passengers looked about them to try to spot the celebrity at their mercy in the confined space. Alex, who hated this sort of thing, shrank down into his seat. Olivia stared fixedly out of the window. Freddie exchanged a word with Caroline across the aisle and Alex thought he had got away with it until Captain Evans emerged from the flight deck, asked the chief steward where the man of the moment was sitting and came down for a friendly chat.

Once Alex's cover was blown, passengers began to struggle past the cabin crew's trolleys to talk to him, shake his hand and ask for his autograph. Alex politely introduced them to his wife and his team's owner, "the man who makes it all possible."

But like all celebrity hunters they were not interested in anyone or anything other than the chosen one, the one they had heard about, read about, but above all felt they knew personally because they had seen him on the television screen in their living room.

Alex was blokeish with the male fans, agreeing with the more gullible ones that it was, indeed, a shame that Teo-Nicolas had crashed on the last lap. Some of them went back to their seats wondering why his wife was so po-faced and whether they ought to know who that smashing dark-haired beauty was, sitting just across the aisle. Perhaps she was an actress whose name they couldn't remember.

A way of life is not easily abandoned and even though his wife was sitting next to him and his lover was only a few feet away, Alex could not resist treating the prettier women to a little sexual *frisson*. He smiled and exchanged pleasantries with each one and signed whatever dedications they wanted. But on handing back their pens and pieces of paper, he looked disturbingly deep into their eyes. He was not only stripping them naked but visualising them in some of the more submissive female postures in the *Kama Sutra*. One or two went back to their seats blushing and smiling nervously to themselves, but the bolder spirits relished the tingle of sexual excitement and wished his wife hadn't been there so that they could have got his phone number as well as his autograph.

6

Alex lost patience with the A303 when it ran out of dual carriageway at Stonehenge and was happy to take the A344 towards Chitterne. This was army country with its tank ranges, Bulford with its barracks, Tidworth famous for its old tattoo, Larkhill, home of the gunners. Driving through Shrewton he could visualise troops of the incomparable Sixth Airborne Division being put through their paces 35 years ago in readiness for securing the flank on D-Day.

He preferred the M3 as being less heavily policed than the M4 and did his best not to call undue attention to the silver Mercedes SL 450. He used the outer lane as little as possible and tried to keep his motorway speed to 90-ish.

Driving as fast as the road, the conditions and weather allowed, there was no need to seek undue thrills, but a sweeping downhill dip with no turnings might be taken at 130 mph while a busy street would be negotiated at 15 to 20 mph if need be. His eyes were never still, missing nothing, reading the road ahead, watching for potential hazards and conning his mirrors. Terrified at first, Olivia had learned to relax and realise that it was speed in the wrong hands, the wrong place and the wrong time that caused danger on the roads, not when an expert was at the wheel.

Deep in their own thoughts, they spoke little on the journey to Sutton Manor, the Georgian house near Warminster Olivia's father had given them for a wedding present. They were greeted on the doorstep by Mrs Porter, their housekeeper. "I saw you comin' up the drive. So I got him to hold on. It's Alex's Dad on the phone."

"What does he want?"

"How should I know? He wants to talk to you."

"He would do, wouldn't he?" muttered Alex as he left the two women to get the luggage out of the car and scrunched across the gravel to the front door.

He picked up the phone in the hall. "Hi, Dad!"

"Alex? Are you all right?"

"Fine, Dad. How are you?"

"I've been worried sick. I don't really expect to pick up my Times and see pictures of my son looking as though he's being carried off a battlefield."

"It was in The Times as well was it? We've only seen the Telegraph." He was still on the race winner's high which could last for days. This heady euphoria of victory was like being slightly drunk on champagne all the time. "Anyway, Dad, it's always nice to hear from you. But since when have you been reading the sports pages?"

"You know I don't as a rule but it seems the only way of finding out what my son's up to. Are you all right?"

"Of course I'm all right. I've just driven down here from Heathrow, haven't I?"

"You looked terrible in those pictures."

"I was just knackered that's all. Heat stroke and dehydration and I passed out for a few moments. It may've looked bad but that's the power of the press. It's just that Monaco in the heat is a damn tiring race anyway and the last thing you need at the end of it is to have to push your bloody car to the line. I just conked out. Fainted. Had a fit of the vapours. End of story. Honest, Dad, that's all there was to it."

"Are you sure?"

"How many more times do I have to tell you? I'm fine. I won the race didn't I?"

"That's your first victory this year isn't it?"

"Yeah. And for bloody ages. I'm really enjoying it."

"I'm very glad for you, Alex. I need to catch up on all your news and the pictures in the paper this morning gave me a jolt, I can tell you. Why don't we have lunch?"

"Love to, Dad. But it'll have to be in the next day or two. Races are every fortnight at this time of year and I'm rushed off my feet."

"My club or yours?"

This was a routine they both rather enjoyed before their very occasional meetings. Charles Bastyan, a long serving Conservative back bench MP who had recently been made a life peer, would propose the Carlton. Alex would say it was 'full of old political fogies' and suggest the RAC, which his father would dismiss as 'The Chauffeur's Arms.' They would then end up opting for neutral ground and going to a restaurant. This was Lord Bastyan's turn, so he chose Rules in Covent Garden. As a family solicitor-cum-politician, he daringly liked to think of himself as being in the tradition of writers, lawyers, actors and artists who had frequented London's oldest restaurant since 1798. He was a self-contained, reserved man and Rules was his idea of the sort of establishment that would also appeal to a sporting son.

"Rules it is then," said Alex. "See you there, Wednesday at 1 o'clock."

* * *

Charles Bastyan chose potted shrimps and rack of lamb while Alex started with smoked salmon and had cod with Welsh rarebit for his main course.

"I shan't have anything but sparkling water but don't let that inhibit you, Dad. I like the way they list wines from North America, South Africa, Australia and New Zealand as being from the former colonies. Great sense of style!"

"I agree. I'm in the Lords this afternoon so I'll join you."

After a lull as they enjoyed their food, Alex broke the awkward silence. Other men seemed to have pleasant enough relationships with fathers they saw once in a blue moon, but he was ill as ease with his. It was just that they didn't meet on any level, intellectual or sporting. He had no childhood memories of bucket-and-spade holidays with a genial father acting as chief castle architect and ice cream supplier. His father was not unkind, indeed, he could scarcely ever remember him raising his voice, but he had been a remote figure, encountered on school holidays and seeming little different from a benign housemaster.

"Tell me, Dad," he said at last. "What's triggered this sudden interest in my career? It's not as if you were a motor racing buff and followed it closely."

Having reached the stage of life where he had much more past than future to contemplate, Charles Bastyan knew he had neglected his son. He had jumped through the obligatory upper middle class hoops and sent him to expensive schools, but he had never been able to communicate with the strong willed little boy who had always insisted on doing everything his way. He had never been able to give what every son craves from a father, his undivided time and attention.

"I'm desperately sorry you feel like that, Alex," he said. "I never meant to be an uncaring father. I know I never gave you the love and attention you deserved but I was just sleep walking through life in my own unhappiness. I just never got over your mother's death. After all these years I never have."

"I know, Dad," he lied. Like many people without happy childhood memories to dwell on, Alex lived entirely for the present and future. To a child, a remote father is not beset with problems and anguish, and as a teenager he had scarcely given his one-parent family a thought. It was just the way things were. All he had wanted to do was to get away from the gloomy Edwardian house in Wimbledon where his father lived alone.

Looking round Rules, all high ceilings with its mirrors and pictures and prints of actors, writers and politicians, Alex knew he'd done his father an injustice all these years. The old boy had been soldiering on, doing his stuff on the back benches after putting in a morning at the law firm and all the time he had been under a burden of grief he couldn't share.

All he had as compensation was a son he didn't get on with and never really understood. Alex resolved to try to keep in touch more often and be a bit nicer to a father who'd had a pretty miserable life. In childhood and during school holidays Alex and his father had never discussed his mother. Charles Bastyan could never bring himself to talk about her to his son.

"It must've been so much worse for you to lose her," Alex said at last. "Kids are tough little buggers and I guess I always felt that what you've never had you don't miss."

In a rare fatherly gesture, Charles Bastyan reached across and shyly placed a pale palm, soft as a woman's, over his son's strong bronzed hand resting on the white linen. Alex looked up sharply. As reticent in his own way, he was wary of any physical contact – except with almost every attractive woman he met.

Not for the first time, he wondered how his father had ever coped with the glad-handing, elbow gripping and soft-soaping during all those years as an MP. And as for having to kiss babies when electioneering... The sheer absurdity of the notion made him smile as he met his father's affectionate gaze.

"Your mother would've been very proud of you – as I am," Charles Bastyan said, removing his hand after a couple of pats and a gentle squeeze. He glanced swiftly round the busy restaurant in case any of the other diners might have known him and witnessed such an un-English gesture.

"Thanks for that Dad. Still, it would be nice if you could come to the British Grand Prix at Silverstone in July. As you were. On second thoughts, don't! I was damn lucky to win at Monaco. We've got the faster circuits coming up like Silverstone, Hockenheim, the Osterreichring and Monza which don't suit us. I'd be lucky to pick up one point, let alone win."

Charles Bastyan had little idea what his son was talking about. He tried to take an interest, if only to be able to answer questions from friends and colleagues. The whole thing baffled him. Alex had first disappointed him by rejecting the law as a profession. Then he hadn't made a career of the army and got involved in this dangerous motor racing business.

Why couldn't the boy have been a cricketer and played for England at Lord's? That was something he could have understood as an MCC member but his son had been hopeless at team games and excelled only at athletics and gym. Worst of all in his father's eyes, Alex had married badly. Olivia would pass muster because she had been sent to a decent school but her parents, Stanley and Edna Heyworth, had struck Charles Bastyan as Birmingham *nouveau riche* and not his cup of tea.

This had led to a distinct coolness between father and son for some years. Alex had called his father a terrible old snob, reminding him that these days people were judged on who they were, and not on how they spoke or what they looked like. Stan was a highly successful Midlands industrialist who could buy up the Bastyans umpteen times over – if he could be bothered. Just because someone's accent wasn't public school, it didn't mean they were dim or unworthy. Besides, there must be plenty of people in the House who didn't have plums in their mouths. You didn't think any the less of them provided they talked sense.

He had tried to get his father to understand that motor racing was a democratic business. It didn't matter where you came from – although it did help to have money. Lots of it. Stan had sponsored him with hard cash while his own father had shown not the slightest interest in his new career.

Charles Bastyan gradually became reconciled. The turning point was when he started reading about his son in The Times and people kept asking him questions. He now realised he had sired a sporting celebrity instead of the solicitor he expected. But the pictures from the Monaco Grand Prix had shaken him.

"I wish you'd give it up, my boy," he said, putting down his knife and fork.

"Give it up? When I've just won Monaco. You must be potty, Dad. I'm on a high but I know it won't last. In my heart of hearts I know I finished first rather than won. I only won because a lot of guys dropped out in front of me. But I must admit I've realised I've got to start thinking about it. I'm getting old."

"You're only 36!"

"That's old when you're not winning all the time."

"Promise me you'll think about it."

"I already have."

Charles Bastyan changed the subject. "There's no chance of my becoming a grandfather, I suppose?"

"'Fraid not, Dad. That takes two people to be in the same bed at the same time with the same object in view. We never seem to be able to get round to it. Olivia's busy with her show jumping and I've got my hands full of Formula One.

"I see. You're being sensible, not starting a family while you're both still so busy in your sports...."

"You could say that, Dad." What Alex couldn't say was that he had never considered having children with Olivia or any of the many other women he had slept with. Only with Caroline. The least paternal of men, he could now actually imagine having children with his best friend's wife. Caroline had once whispered to him how she longed to bear his children. What beautiful daughters they could have. And the sons wouldn't be too bad either – Caroline's genes might give them a bit more height than the Bastyans enjoyed. These were dangerous thoughts and it was time to talk of different things.

"How's the House of Lords?" he enquired.

"Fine, thanks. We like to think we enjoy a more reasoned, rational kind of debate without too much party political point scoring."

"You must be dead chuffed to be there in your old age."

"Dead chuffed? What sort of expression is that?" The crusty old lawyer-politician was never very far away.

"Don't try sounding like an unworldly High Court judge, Dad. You know what chuffed means. I was only trying to say it must be a great honour to be in the House of Lords."

"It depends on how you get there. Inheritance is one way and no particular merit attaches to that. That's luck."

Alex interrupted with a mischievous grin, "What about good breeding? Don't forget that."

Charles Bastyan smiled. "Of course. That's fine for some. But to be sent there because you're an ex-Cabinet Minister or achieved great things is something else. I'm under no illusion about why I was kicked upstairs. It was only because my ultra-safe seat was wanted for some young Turk from Central Office, destined for high office. I understand that from all the advantage and experience of his 23 years he had been advising three Cabinet Ministers. I think I can use the word 'advise' advisedly in this context," said Lord Bastyan with a wry smile.

Alex laughed. "Wow! That's the first time I've ever heard you make a funny."

"No? Am I really such a boring old bugger?"

"Of course not. But you need to relax a bit. Enjoy yourself. Take more holidays and get away from it all on a cruise, or something. There's no knowing who you might meet." Alex was about to say, 'Join a dating agency' but knew his father would be shocked beyond measure. "You really ought to let your hair down."

With a faint, rueful smile Charles Bastyan passed a hand over his shiny dome.

"What hair?"

"Metaphorical follicles in your case, Dad. My God! A terrible thought's just struck me. Do you think I'll be as bald as you when I'm your age?"

"Who knows? Your grandfather had a good head of hair when he was 70. Maybe the male baldness gene comes down through the female line. You may be lucky."

"God! I hope so. I seem to be holding my own at the moment," Alex said, patting his short, wiry thatch.

"How's Olivia?" asked Charles Bastyan.

"Same as ever," he replied.

This caught him off guard. He knew his father quite liked Olivia and he also knew what he owed to her forbearance. He had betrayed her left, right and centre but she kept her own counsel. He didn't love her but he wasn't going to rubbish her.

"She's a dark horse. She broods but then she's got a lot to brood about."

When he had time to think about it, he wondered whether Olivia was a plotter as well. But wasn't it only obsessive women, desperately in love, who planned revenge against unfaithful husbands? He had never thought she cared enough for him to bother.

"I'm afraid," he continued, "ours is a marriage of long absences and even longer silences. We each do our own things. I'm the world's worst husband, I guess."

"I expect things'll improve when you can be together more," Charles Bastyan said. "Why," he inquired mildly, "do you have to use Americanisms? Your conversation is peppered with 'guys' and expressions like 'I guess'. I've noticed a general sloppiness in your speech, my boy. I realise all you young fellows who've had an expensive education seem to feel the need to talk down these days, as if you were ashamed of it. But there's no need to do it to me, you know."

"Sorry, Dad. That's Formula One for you. It's international and classless, somehow mid-Atlantic, like showbiz – there I go again – and the pop world – the, er milieu of popular music.

It's rolling in money but it's a meritocracy. It doesn't matter who you are or where you come from. As long as you can deliver. But it's a young man's game, Dad, and it eats people, chews them up and spits them out. On that charming note, what can I say but thanks for lunch, it's been great seeing you again and I promise to watch the diction. Mustn't let Cliftonbury down – I carry the old school colours on my helmet, did I tell you?"

Alex took a final swig from his water glass, stood up and shook his father's hand. "Must go, Dad. Got a busy week. I promised to look in at Bracknell on the way home. You stay and finish your coffee. Give my love to their Lordships. We must do this more often. G-bye."

Walking down Maiden Lane, he couldn't remember when he'd ever had a longer, more intimate, family conversation with his father. But there had been no point in mentioning Caroline. A man who'd spent 30 years grieving and never re-married would have scant sympathy for a married son who claimed to love another man's wife.

7

"Good God, Alex! What's up?" asked Mike Morgan. He had just put his head round the door of the Tremayne team motorhome parked behind the pits at Spa-Francorchamps in the Belgian Ardennes.

With the top half of his logo-bedecked fireproof overalls round his waist and a dejected expression, Bastyan was nobody's idea of a Formula One hero as he sat slumped in a corner, drinking tepid coffee from a plastic cup.

"Come in, Mike. There's nobody here but me and my problems."

"Can this be the Monarch of Monaco I see before me all alone and palely loitering?"

"Stop taking the piss, you old Welsh windbag. You know I didn't win that race. I didn't even finish first, I inherited the damn thing and even then the bloody car couldn't get me to the line without a push. Get yourself a beer, by the way. There's some in the fridge."

Morgan helped himself and sat down on the bench seat opposite.

"Care to tell Uncle Mike all about it?"

"Off the record?"

"Of course."

"No hidden tape recorders?"

"Cross my heart."

"You buggers don't have hearts. You'd sell your own mothers for a good story."

"Come off it, Alex! When've I ever let you down or betrayed a confidence?"

"You haven't, old boy. I'm sorry. But I wouldn't trust some of those Fleet Street fellers further than I could throw 'em."

"Don't be too hard on those boyos. Alex. They've got a job to do. The main difference between the daily guys and us chaps on the mags is that we're enthusiasts for the sport through and through, while they're devotees of journalism. They're always having to look for the big stories because they have to compete for space in their own papers against all the other sports.

"We don't have to do that and we know every word we write gets in. But that doesn't make us uncritical lapdogs, with the Fleet Street guys being the watchdogs. We'll bark all right when there's something to bark about. Such as the way the ticket buying punter gets treated, for starters. But what's on *your* mind, Alex?"

"Every bloody thing. I'm in a team I've lost confidence in, I've got a team-mate I could cheerfully strangle, my love life's a disaster, oh, and I nearly forgot – my marriage is on the rocks. Apart from that, everything's fine," he said bitterly. "I can take the cockpit trouble, I can take the problems at home, but what really gets to me is not seeing her. For the first time in my life I've discovered what it is to miss another human being. There's nothing worse than losing the person who means most in the world to you when she's not even yours to lose. Hell! She's married to my oldest friend."

"It's Caroline Tremayne?"

Alex nodded. "God knows I love that woman, but I haven't

seen her since Monaco. I've bought peace in our time at home by saying I wouldn't see her but *she's* giving me the elbow and that's more than I can stand. The trouble is I hurt her. I hit her but I had to. Don't get me wrong, Mike. I don't make a habit of socking women but it just had to be done. I'm not proud of it but we were in her and Freddie's bedroom at the Hermitage the night before the Monaco race.

"The four of us – that's Freddie and Caroline, Olivia and me –had been out on a modest toot before an early bed. Olivia was the first to call it a day and went back to our room in the Hôtel de Paris. Freddie wanted to stay in the casino and have a natter with one of his old mates so that left Caroline and me. All this is strictly *entre nous,* off the record?"

Morgan nodded. "Of course."

"The inevitable happened. We went back to her hotel room and made love. It's a helluva thing to say but I'm afraid my body might've been on the job but my mind wasn't. I was worried sick. For starters, Freddie was due back any minute. We'd no idea how much longer he was going to stay at the casino. It could've been five hours or five minutes for all we knew.

"Don't forget it was past midnight and the race was only about 14 hours away. Practice had been a nightmare. My car was handling like a drunken sailor on shore leave and I was on the eighth row, two behind the dreaded Thibault. Much as I adore Caroline I was not at my best. Perhaps I didn't satisfy her. I don't know. All I knew was that I had to get the hell out of there, try and get some kip in my own bed and work out some sort of strategy for the race. As I figured it, the only thing to be said for the back of the grid was that I should be able to avoid the almost compulsory pile-up at Ste Devote. I just had to get my clothes on and get out of that room. Can you imagine what would've happened if Freddie had come back and found us? But she was all worked up - you know what women are like, bless 'em. She wanted me to make love to her all night and to hell with the consequences. It was madness but she just didn't seem to care. To get her to see sense I had to slap her – pretty hard I'm afraid.

"I see," said Morgan thoughtfully. "If I were you, Alex, I wouldn't worry too much about that slap. I'd say it has damn-all to do with the, er, estrangement. Some women even enjoy being knocked about. Not that I'm suggesting she's like that. My reading of the situation – for what it's worth – is that she's more pissed-off that you turned her down sexually. She was offering you her all but you didn't want it."

"Hell hath no fury, eh? But I wasn't scorning her, for Pete's sake. Surely she could see that we couldn't do it again with her husband's foot almost on the ruddy stair? Couldn't she see it was only expediency and that I was acting in both our best interests?"

"I doubt it, boyo. Women's minds don't work like that. Not when sex rears its lovely head. They may take longer to get worked up than we do, but when they are, heaven help the male of the species who can't or won't deliver. The important thing is that you're sure she really loves you?"

"I'm sure she does."

"Well then, she's the one who doesn't give a toss. She wanted Freddie to find the two of you together. She was prepared to face the music, be caught *in flagrante* and bring your love affair out into the open. To force the issue. You flunked it."

"Of course!" said Alex, "you clever bugger. I suppose I was just on autopilot and not giving her the attention she deserved. I remember now. She said she'd leave Freddie for me and I just made some facetious remark. It must've broken her heart. But having it out with The Husband, my team boss, don't forget, was the last thing I needed a few hours before a grand prix. But right now, if that's the only way of seeing her again, I feel like going straight up to Freddie and – "

"Is that what you really want, Alex? To break up two marriages, even if there aren't any kids involved. I've been through a divorce and I know what it's like."

"But I can't go on like this, Mike. What the hell'm I to do?"

"Nothing *pre-cipi-tate,* boyo, if I were you. If she loves you as much as you think, she'll find a way of working something out. Women are much better at these things than we are. She's not going to let you go. Old Mother Morgan predicts that you'll be together before the end of the year. But get the racing season over first. Don't let it interfere with your driving."

"Nothing precipitate? You're right, Mike. I'm a racing driver, for Gawd's sake." He put down his cup, got to his feet, zipped up his overalls. "Right now I'm going back to the Val d'Amblève – not a bad little pub that – but do you know what I'm going to do tomorrow? I'm going to wring that fucking car's neck. And I'm going to drive my balls off for the rest of the season."

"You bet. Sock it to 'em!" said Morgan.

* * *

"You don't know how lucky you are to be here," Mike Morgan told Pete Randall. They were sitting in the press box before the start of the race on Sunday.

"I bless the day I joined, but why here in particular?" asked Randall.

"Because, boyo, Spa is one of the great circuits, not to be mentioned in the same breath with all these new piddling built-for-TV, no-overtaking tracks that are becoming all the rage. It's on a par with the old Nurburgring and Monza. Even though it's had to be modified for safety reasons, much of its glory remains.

"While the rest of us were sweating it out in the interim at strange places like Zolder, and even Nivelles, you were spared all that. For Nivelles we used to stay in Brussels and hack out to the circuit which was a bit of a bind. The only thing to be said for Zolder was that it was close to the motorway and the best place to stay was just over the Dutch border at Maastricht. A nice old town with some interesting sex shops. You know what the Dutch are like."

"I've never been to a sex shop," said Randall, almost wistfully.

"I don't suppose you've ever had a woman either."

"It depends on what you mean by *have*. For heaven's sake, Mike, We're not here to discuss my sex life," said Randall blushing.

"Of course not. We'll come back to that uninteresting topic later. For the moment I'm making good the gaps in your motor racing education. Of course, 1966 was the important year when half the field crashed on the very first lap, because the circuit was wet in some parts and not in others. Cars were aquaplaning off all over the place.

"That's what led to the circuit being shortened and the introduction of all sorts of safety measures and medical facilities. There've been some great races here like the duel in 1970 between Pedro Rodriguez in the BRM and Chris Amon who set the fastest lap at 152 mph in a March. Those were the days when we used to stand at the Masta kink to watch and listen to who was taking it absolutely flat and who was lifting off. Great days, boyo.

"Not only that, this part of the world is interesting historically. Did you realise that just round here marks as far as the Germans got in von Rundstedt's last big push in the winter of 1944. Crafty old bugger, everybody thought this wasn't good tank country, but he sliced through the Yanks like a knife through butter until he was stopped in these parts.

"Monty was called in to take control and always liked to give the impression he won the Battle of the Bulge all by himself but what really did it was the Gerries outrunning their supply lines and the weather changing so we could get our planes in the air. Air power is what decides modern warfare, boyo."

Randall looked surprised. "Since when have you been a military expert, Mike?"

"I'm not, no way. But World War Two is one of my interests – not that I fancy myself as a Mastermind contender on it. It's an interest I share with Alex, oddly enough. He and I have spent many a pleasant hour, fighting old battles and arguing the toss about Montgomery's position in the military pantheon."

"When does all this take place then?" asked Randall. He was eager to find out how to get on good terms with as many drivers as possible.

"Here and there. Perhaps in the bar when he and I found ourselves in the same hotel. More often in the Tremayne motorhome on a practice day. Alex always jokes that practice is like warfare – 99 per cent boredom and one percent sheer terror. Had quite a session with him on Friday, as it happens. No, I maintain that Monty was the first PR general who took the trouble to put himself across to the troops instead of just shouting orders at them. They liked that and they also knew that he'd take immense trouble in planning a battle not to squander their lives needlessly.

"I think any view of Monty depends on class. Seeing as I'm a Welsh socialist, I take the private soldier's standpoint while Alex takes the officer's stance that he was a vainglorious, ungentlemanly blighter who could never give anybody else credit and hogged all the limelight for himself. Alex makes the point that Monty had the devil's own luck because he was never first choice for his key appointments. He would never have got the Eighth Army if 'Strafer' Gott hadn't been killed in an air crash and he wasn't first choice for Normandy either.

"I counter that by saying that luck was a part of generalship – Napoleon always wanted to know if his generals were lucky – and that anyway, when Monty did get the job, he always delivered. The trouble with Alex is, he's an ex-Para and he can never forgive Monty for Arnhem and the destruction of the First Airborne Division. That's where I always tell him he's being unfair.

"All right, Arnhem was a military disaster and Monty ordered it but you have to look at these things in the context of the time. The Germans had been running ever since they were kicked out of Normandy. Paris and Brussels had been liberated and the war seemed to be nearly over. For once Monty acted out of character. Everybody criticised him for being too slow and cautious so he'd do something really bold. It very nearly came off.

"It only didn't because he didn't put a big enough rocket up the backsides of the troops of Second Army who were supposed to join up with the Paras. Instead of pressing on hell for leather the advance would stop for tea to be brewed-up, so Alex says. He reckons if old 'Blood and Guts' Patton had been in command the relief force would've got through.

"Meanwhile, the poor sods of First Airborne were being wiped out. No, I can see why he's not pro-Monty but I don't think Alex's being altogether fair. Well, boyo, lecture's over. I see they've got the five-minute board out on the starting grid and we'll soon have some action. Who do you fancy?"

"It should be Johnny Abati in the McColl on form but I'd've thought a fast track like this should suit the V-12 Ferraris - it looks a benefit for the Italians. My money's on Antoniazzi or Morandini," said Randall.

"Well done! Got it in one. I couldn't do better myself. You're learning fast," said Morgan. "And how about Alex?"

"He should be in the points. Possibly third, more likely fourth, I'd say. Something sure got into him for second practice – pulling up half a dozen places and getting himself on to the second row!"

"Now I wonder what that could've been," said Morgan with a smile.

8

"What a spectacle, boyo!" bellowed Morgan as the cars streaked off the grid. Then, undertrays striking sparks off the track surface as suspensions bottomed, the field swarmed up the hill from Eau Rouge with a blast of sound that made the ground tremble.

"And everyone got away cleanly, too," said Randall. "Alex was well up there behind the two Ferraris and Johnny's McColl."

"We grumble about it but thank God we've got TV here," said Morgan. "They've cut the circuit length from eight miles to four but without it we wouldn't have a clue what was happening on the rest of the track. Can you imagine what it was like at the Nürburgring – all 14 miles of it, when you had to wait seven minutes for them to come round again? There was almost time to pop out for a drink or take the dog for a walk. At least these days you can see what's going on elsewhere. They're climbing up to Les Combes now."

Two minutes 10 seconds later the field came streaming down from La Source, past the pits uphill towards Raidillon, led by the Ferraris.

"Hang on a minute," said Randall, "Alex wasn't there! That's rotten luck on the first lap."

"He's in the pits. It's on the telly. They're changing a wheel. And making a right fuck-up by the look of it – all falling over themselves. He's been in there 45 seconds. That's disastrous. Freddie Tremayne and Big Mac'll be tearing their hair out."

"Perhaps they should've been practising more tyre changes?" said Randall.

"Here comes Alex now, out of the pits. Half a lap behind. I bet the air's blue inside that blue and gold helmet of his. I wouldn't care to be any of that pit crew when Alex gets hold of them after the race."

Taking crafty peeks at Morgan's immaculate lap chart, Randall brought his own untidy effort up to date. With the two Ferraris pulling away from Johnny Abati's McColl, the surprise on the leader board was the form of Alan Mason in the Lotus who had caught up to fourth with Juan Baltieri fifth in the Brabham.

To the delight of the British press corps, the Belgian TV producer had the good sense to return frequently to Bastyan's climb back through the field. By half distance he was right up behind his team-mate Thibault who was refusing to give up his ninth place.

Along every straight Bastyan slipstreamed Thibault's car, pulling out at the last minute to out-brake him for the corner. But the little Frenchman was having none of it. This was the best part of the race, two team-mates reputed to be scarcely on speaking terms, conducting a grudge fight for lap after lap.

"Looks like some bumping and boring going on here," said Morgan who had deputed Randall to keep the lap chart while he monitored the Bastyan-Thibault contest on the nearest television set. "If this were horse racing, boyo, there'd be a stewards' inquiry."

"What's the rule on it?" asked Randall.

"Bit of a grey area. But basically the guy who's got his

nose ahead on the racing line has the right to the corner, and the other driver has to give him best and back off."

"Why doesn't the other chap go round the outside?" asked Randall.

"It wastes time. The shortest distance between two points is a straight line and the whole object of quick driving is to straighten out the corners. The guy who goes round off the racing line doesn't get very far. I can see Alex has had about enough of this. Watch this bit now. The camera's on both of them as they come up to this corner. Thibault's fractionally ahead but Alex's got his nearside wheels in between the Banger's offside ones. There's cool for you, man. I swear they're not touching anywhere. What precision, placing the car to an inch. Strewth!

"He's driving Thibault right off the track without even touching him. The poor little bugger had nowhere to go, chickened out, and to avoid hitting Alex's car, he's in the boonies. That's the most fantastic bit of driving I ever saw – pushing someone off without so much as a tap. What finesse! What a driver. He sure takes no prisoners."

"But that's illegal, isn't it?" asked Randall.

"Of course, but difficult to prove without any actual contact. But you can bet your last Belgian franc that little Thibault will scream blue murder and squeal all the way to FIA in Paris demanding to have Alex tarred and feathered, unfrocked, disbarred, cashiered, castrated and anything else unpleasant he can think of."

"Meanwhile," said Randall, "Alex is charging off after the leaders. He obviously won't catch them now but he might get a point for sixth place."

"Don't underestimate him. He could do better than that when he's fired up like this. He's driving like a man inspired. Anyway, what's been happening to the leaders while our Alex has been thrilling the crowds and frightening the frogs?"

Randall consulted his lap chart. "I make it Morandini in the lead in the second Ferrari – Antoniazzi's engine blew up.

Johnny's out as well with gearbox trouble. We've got a Brit in second place with Alan Mason in the Lotus. That's great. Then there's Juan Baltieri third in the Brabham, Hugo Falcus fourth in the Tyrrell, Bengt Christensen fifth in the second McLaren and Harald Kastner sixth in the Fantino-Mostyn."

"Where's Alex?" demanded Morgan.

As Randall searched frantically through his columns, a shout went up in the press box. All over the room people stood up and craned to get a better view of the TV sets. The camera was lingering on a blue and green car with its nose buried in the crash barrier and listing to one side. Trackside marshals were running towards it, one of them lugging an extinguisher. Fortunately there were no tell-tale wisps of smoke. But there was no sign of movement in the cockpit for half a minute. Eventually the driver could be seen trying to undo his safety harness and struggling to get out.

"Who is it?"

"It's got to be Bastyan – that's not a McColl," said someone. The camera then panned back down the track tracing gouge marks in the surface. Before it came to rest, Morgan gasped. "Jeez! He's had a wheel come off!"

9

Having focused for a second or two on the little front wheel jammed up against the guardrail, and assuming that the driver was in one piece, the Belgian TV producer lost interest and redirected his coverage to the race leaders.

Out of sight, lying with his back against the Armco, Alex waited for his head to clear. This must be like being on the receiving end of Muhammad Ali's knock out punch, he thought. His brain seemed somehow to have rotated inside his skull, inside the helmet, with the force of the impact as his neck had snapped forward and then back. His helmet might even have hit the steering wheel as the belts flexed slightly. He couldn't be sure of anything.

There had been no warning. No time to do anything but brake, and brace himself. He had been accelerating in third gear out of Rivage at about 130 mph when the car gave a sickening lurch to the right and the offside front wheel bowled away on its own. He had fought desperately for a few seconds to keep it straight but, as if in slow motion, the car had slewed to the right, jerked as the suspension dug into the grass verge, and then struck the Armco.

His senses were at such a pitch that he could smell the disturbed earth and grass, and then he was conscious of little but the buffeting and the graunching metal, of the light grey of the barrier streaking past at head height for such an eternity that it seemed the contact must shave the side of the tub down to nothing. At last the car had come to a stop, and there was no sound but the ticking of hot metal.

After the marshals had helped him out of the wreck, over the barrier and then removed his helmet and balaclava, Bastyan lay still on the grass. Every part of his body ached. The shock of the impact with the Armco, glancing blow though it was, seemed to have been transmitted up the very bone marrow of his braced legs. The pain reminded him of the heavy parachute landing when he had broken his ankle.

But he had been twenty then and now he was nearer forty and there came a time, however fit you were, when the body found it harder to cope with shocks. He blessed the Willans harness which had pinned him like a butterfly on a card to the engine bulkhead. He felt sore and would doubtless have enormous bruises round the shoulders, pelvis and upper thighs where the straps had held him down and saved him from injury.

After a few moments waiting for his mental screen to clear, the world about him to come into focus and make sense again, he got to his feet gingerly with the aid of one of the marshals. He could stand, even if his legs and his right ankle did ache like hell. Ignoring the marshals' pleas that he should wait to be examined by a doctor, Alex picked up his helmet and set out to jog the mile back to the pits with his teeth gritted and his heart full of fury.

* * *

With his tabloid responsibilities in mind, Mike Morgan decided that whatever was happening to the leaders of this particular Belgian GP the real human interest story of the race would develop when Alex Bastyan got back to the Tremayne pits. Leaving Randall to maintain the lap chart, he made his way to the pit lane.

In between watching Bastyan's progress through the field, Freddie Tremayne and Jim MacGregor had been doing their best to placate a furious Teo-Nicolas Thibault.

"Aleex poosh me off ze zirqueet, Freddie," Thibault kept repeating. "You must do sumzing about eem. Ee could ave kill me."

Freddie, more concerned about his number one driver who could be seriously injured for all he knew, kept murmuring platitudes. "He can't have pushed you very hard the way he's been breaking the lap record until this happened. Now I've got both my bloody cars out. Do give it a rest, Teo-Nicolas, there's a good chap, till we've found out what's happened to Alex."

At that moment Mike Morgan came up.

"I just popped my head in at race control and they say Alex is OK and walking back. I'm surprised they haven't announced it."

"Thank God for that, Mike. Perhaps they did and we missed it. Ah, here he comes now, staggering up the hill. Let's go down to meet him. You'd better stay there, Teo-Nicolas," added Freddie as the little Frenchman started huffing and puffing.

"Where's that bastard Stevens?" bellowed Bastyan before they were in normal earshot. "I want to wring his fucking neck. He sodding near killed me. Get that incompetent cretin off my pit crew, Freddie, because I'm not getting into a car of yours again until that useless bugger's out of my sight."

Tremayne liked to conduct his team's business in such peace and quiet as motor racing ever allowed, instead of fortissimo in public and in front of the press. He took his driver gently by the arm.

"Come on, Alex. Let's go and discuss all this in the motorhome. I'd expect you'd like to sit down anyway. Are you sure we oughtn't to get Sid to have a look at you?"

"I'm all right. But no thanks to your bloody pit crew. They take five minutes to fit a sodding off side front and then they can't even make sure it doesn't come off."

"Have a heart, Alex. We all thought you'd been doing your own bit of wheel banging. I've got Teo-Nicolas jumping up and down saying that you pushed him off. It's too bad. I really can't have my drivers fighting among themselves like alley cats."

Alex snorted. "I've got enough on my plate without bringing that little French prat into it! Besides I never touched him. If he hasn't the sense to back off and keep out of his team leader's way, he deserves everything he gets. We'll deal with him later – he's nothing but a bloody nuisance. This Stevens is a potential killer. Can you get him over to the motorhome right away, Freddie?"

"I think Mac had better sit in on this," said Tremayne. "After all, Terry's one of his chaps." Mike Morgan, who had been trying to make himself as inconspicuous as possible, knew there was no way he was going to be allowed into what was a private team discussion. He pushed off, doubting whether he'd be able to get any sort of statement later, but at least he had satisfied himself that Alex was OK with his temper in fine form. The Tremayne team's involvement might be over but there was still a motor race going on.

A cross between hangdog and defiant, Terry Stevens was summoned to the motorhome for the hearing that Alex wanted to conduct like a court martial. In theory, a split-pin should make it impossible for a wheel to come off the hub. Apart from the general incompetence of the long pit stop, the issue, as he saw it, depended on whether or not, in the heat of the moment - with all four wheels being changed as a precaution - the split-pin had been forgotten on the offside front.

Stevens, who had been responsible for that side of the car,

insisted that it had been fitted. Alex said it couldn't've been or the wheel wouldn't come adrift. Unwisely, Stevens countered this by saying that Alex could've damaged the wheel himself. This produced a volcanic explosion of temper and denial.

"The way I drive is my bloody business. We all have to keep our cool with the nightmare of mechanical failure. But fucking hopeless pit work is something up with which I will not fucking put!"

It was simply a question of one man's word against another's and the truth of the matter would probably never be known. Freddie and Mac exchanged glances.

"Do you mind waiting outside for a few moments, Terry," said Tremayne.

"I know what you're after, Alex," said MacGregor. "You want me to sack Terry. I can't do that. I know he's an ornery cuss at times and often his own worst enemy but I can't sack him for one mistake, specially one that hasn't even been proved to my satisfaction. Mechanics are the unsung heroes of Formula One, Alex. You know that. We flog'em to death and don't pay 'em half as much as we should. Quite frankly I don't know why half of them put up with it ... Terry's an odd ball I admit, but he's been with us since Formula Three days. Besides, he's got three kids.

"I don't care how many kids he's got. I just want him off my pit crew.

"Be reasonable, Alex. Those guys'd been up half the night rebuilding the car Teo-Nicolas dinged in practice yesterday. And they are under pressure during pit stops, don't forget that."

"Pressure? I'll give'em fucking pressure," said Alex, his face still white with fury. "I've got enough to contend with on the track without having my efforts sabotaged by my own bleedin' mechanics. It's either him or me. I'm not joking guys. I'm not getting into another car of yours that Stevens has so much as laid a grimy finger on."

Tremayne and MacGregor exchanged helpless glances.

"You'd better ask Terry to come in again, Mac," said Freddie.

One look told Terry Stevens how the land lay. "He's out to get me, Mr Tremayne – it's not your fault," he said.

"I'm afraid you'd better push off," said Freddie, ever the conciliator. "Till things cool down a bit."

Without waiting for anything more to be said, Stevens turned away. Pausing in the doorway of the motorhome he looked straight at Alex and hissed through uneven teeth: "I'll get you for this, Bastyan. You're the biggest fuckin' bastard I ever met."

Alex gave him a mirthless smile. "That's what they all say, Terry. How could I possibly deny it?"

* * *

As Alex went over to his car he found Teo-Nicolas standing in front of it, as if defying him to leave the paddock.

"You are bastard, Aleex – you nearly kill me," he said quivering with rage.

"Oh God, not you as well. We've just dealt with one unsuccessful case of attempted murder. You haven't seen Terry Stevens by the way? I wanted to have a word with him now we're all trying to calm down a bit."

"You pooshed me off ze zirqueet!"

"I did no such thing! Show me the mark on your car. If you can't keep the bloody thing on the island that's your fault, not mine. You should've got the hang of F1 by now. If not, why not piss-off back to F3?"

He was tired, on edge and the reaction from the shunt was setting in. All he wanted to do was to get back to the Val d'Amblève, have a bath and try to relax.

"I am from Marseilles," said Thibault with all the menace

of his five feet two inches. "I know some 'eavy men who can do zings to you, Aleex."

"'Eavy men who do zings? What *are* you threatening me with? Oh, you mean heavies? Do calm down, Teo-Nicolas. Everyone's heavier than you. In any other sport you'd be given a weight penalty. Now, if you'll excuse me...?"

10

The French Grand Prix has been a moveable feast with many homes but that year at Dijon it was remembered for only one thing – the death of Gianni Abati, the reigning world champion. The results, of course, went down in the record books and the points scored counted towards the world championship. For the record, the race was won by Juan Baltieri of Argentina in a Brabham, with the Brazilian Hector Bonfante second in a McLaren and Abati's countryman, Guy Antoniazzi third in his Ferrari. But the grand prix meeting would really only be recalled and reviled for the loss of a great and popular world champion.

Nobody smiled on the victory podium, the crowd went home quietly and an atmosphere of sadness and despondency hung over the little circuit in the rolling countryside, near the village of Prenois for the entire weekend.

For a country that is so besotted with motor racing, Italy has produced remarkably few world champions. After a good start in 1950 with Giuseppe Farina and Alberto Ascari in 1952 and 1953, there had been no-one till Gianni Abati who had won it four years ago and was the current world champion with two titles to his name. The way things were going, he was expected to collect a third, having 28 points from six races, with wins in South Africa and Long Beach, being second in San Marino and third at Silverstone.

He was idolised in Italy despite never having driven for Ferrari. Both his championships had been won in Peterboro McColl cars which also gave him a big following in Britain. But Gianni - Johnny - Abati enjoyed worldwide admiration with his outgoing personality, while his flashing smile and dark curls gave him hearthrob status with millions of female motor racing fans.

His lifestyle, with a beautiful young blonde English wife and two little children was featured in magazines from Monte Carlo to Mogadishu and he was admired and fêted without envy or rancour wherever he went as an excellent ambassador for the sport.

A policeman's son from Calabria, his first acquaintance with power and speed came from illegally riding his father's official motor cycle late at night. He would wait till the little household was asleep, then creep down and struggle to push the big Ducati along the road till it was out of earshot before firing up the vee twin to go roaring round the countryside.

Entirely self-taught, he rode skilfully, showing all the signs of finesse and courage he was to exhibit later on four wheels on the world stage. His illegal riding, begun at the age of 14 might have gone undiscovered for years if he had not run out of petrol one night, been forced to leave the machine, walk disconsolately home 20 kilometres and confess in the morning. The young Gianni's mother was furious, fearing for her son's life, but his father was secretly proud of the boy.

A frustrated racing motor cyclist himself, he encouraged Gianni to take up the sport as soon as he was old enough. The boy's precocious talent soon brought him to the notice of a wealthy local car dealer with connections in Torino. A job with Fiat then led to one test-driving Ferrari road cars.

Just as the highroad to England is said to be the finest sight for any Scotsman, the budding motor racing driver anywhere in the world finds that Britain with its wealth of circuits, racing schools and events – despite the climate – is the place to acquire his craft. Johnny learned to temper Italian flair and brio with Anglo-Saxon coolness under pressure; to drive like a Latin and think like a Northern European.

Living in uncomfortable digs and existing on landlady's stew, the young Abati soon made his mark in Formula Ford. Within two seasons of coming to England he was European Formula Three champion and had won the prestigious Formula Three curtain-raiser to the Monaco Grand Prix. This led to test driving for McColl where his lap times, often out-stripping those of the contracted team drivers, so impressed Dick McColl that he was in the grand prix team the following season. The rest is motor racing history.

Gianni Abati came to Dijon as the reigning world champion and championship leader, having failed to score points only because of mechanical misfortune at Monaco and Spa. He was fully expected to add the French Grand Prix to his tally of victories and to join the distinguished ranks of triple world champions by the end of the season. But fate decreed otherwise and with shocking finality, his life was to end in a split second.

Having familiarised himself with the circuit and the opposition, Abati would set a fast time and then sit out most of a practice session in his McColl's cockpit, watching other drivers' times on the television monitor placed on the cockpit coaming in front of him. Only if his throne seemed in danger would he set out to put the upstart pretender in his place.

In the last 10 minutes of practice on Friday, Alan Mason in the Lotus had surprisingly recorded a time a few hundredths quicker. There was another session the next day but the weather might change and Abati was taking no chances. He liked to stamp his authority on both practice periods, take the pole position and dictate the race from the front wherever possible.

This was to be no exception and no one thought anything

of it when he roared out on to the circuit with only a few minutes of the session left.

"Johnny's going for a quick one a bit late," remarked the pit lane pundits, preparing to amend their provisional practice lists when the laptime for the green and white McColl was posted. It never was.

Breasting the blind rise on an undemanding corner at 140 mph, Abati was confronted by the Fantino-Mostyn of the Japanese novice Toshiro Watanabe spinning out of control in front of him. Even a world champion's reactions could not save him, and the cars touched. The McColl was deflected into the crash barrier at 90 degrees at a spot where there was no tyre wall to reduce the impact and Abati was killed instantly. Watanabe was unhurt.

* * *

Some part of the great cloud of depression that hung over the little Dijon circuit was taken home by everyone who had been there that fateful weekend. But the disappointment Alex Bastyan felt, at failing to score any points in a race yet again, was completely overshadowed by Johnny's death.

Abati was the individual he admired as a driver and liked as a man above all others. His God-given natural talent sat so lightly on him. It was no big deal that he was invariably so much quicker than anyone else. Equally, there were no sulks and tantrums during the rare times when mechanical troubles prevented him from doing well.

His sunny disposition saw him through the temporary faults till normal service at the head of the field could be resumed. Everything came so easily to him and he was such an unspoiled individual that few could find it in their hearts to begrudge the driver the girls called Gorgeous Gianni his much deserved success. If ever a racing driver could be described as 'much loved' it was Abati.

And now this marvellous man was gone. Wiped out in the blink of an eye in a coming-together with a rent-a-drive novice who had no business in a Formula One field. Watanabe, who had the grace to announce his retirement on the spot, spent the rest of the weekend in tears, telling anyone who would listen that it was his fault.

All this was going through Alex's mind like a record with its needle stuck in a groove as he drove home to Wiltshire from Heathrow. Shouldn't he quit like poor little Tosh, the wannabe who was now a neverwillbe, fated to be remembered only as the other driver involved in Abati's death. If it could happen to Johnny it could happen to anybody. There had been no fatal accidents for four seasons and car and circuit safety was gradually improving. Perhaps they'd all been getting too complacent. McColl cars had a reputation for strength combined with speed, and they were said to make use of some 'demon tweaks' and the use of metals that Dick McColl brought with him from aircraft design. But all this expertise had been unable to save the greatest of them all. If it couldn't save Johnny, then who was safe?

Pulling himself together, he knew that no one in motor racing expected it to be safe. Another thought that had crept weasel-like and insidiously into his mind as soon as the first shock of the news of the tragedy had worn off, now began to surface. Who was going to get the McColl drive? Dick McColl ran a funny outfit with the number one being everything and the number two simply there to make up the numbers. There was no question of the young German, Erwin Schrammer being promoted.

McColl's would be looking for a new number one. Ignoring all other factors, there wasn't a single driver he could think of on a contract that wasn't going to be difficult to break. He wondered whether Dick McColl knew he was only on a gentleman's agreement, handshake basis, with Freddie Tremayne. He doubted it because that was really unprofessional in the days of big deals and managers. Even if approached, he couldn't let Freddie down. Could he? It was out of the question. But the chance of sitting in the world champion's car with its Renault engine ... How could he turn that down? Who could refuse if offered a drive by the sandy little genius of Formula One?

* * *

As soon as he put his key in the lock he remembered that Olivia had told him before he had left for Dijon that she was going to be in Warwickshire this week combining some show jumping with a visit to her parents, Stan and Edna.

There were two notes on the kitchen table. One from Olivia reminding him where she could be contacted and promising to return by Friday. The other was in the barely legible scrawl of their housekeeper, Mrs Porter. It gave a Northampton number and read: PLEASE RING MISTER MAKOLL.

11

Dick McColl, whose team could be compared with the all-time greats of the sport, McLaren and Ferrari – not to mention Lotus – with its mega buck sponsorship from the Peterboro Chemical Corporation, wanted him to call. It could mean only one thing. It must be the Big One. The call to join him.

Few people claimed to have got close enough to know much about McColl, the tight-lipped bachelor and Cambridge-trained engineer who had cut his teeth on supersonic fighter design before turning his hi-tech intellect to Formula One.

He was rumoured to live in some style in Northamptonshire, commuting by helicopter between his home, the factory and endless testing at Silverstone. His private life was a mystery and there was said to be no female in his life, only Formula One. His impact on grand prix racing was immense and even Enzo Ferrari was prepared to admit that McColl, with his engineering ability, his business acumen and his skill at picking drivers was the first among the *garagistas*. This was the ironic tag used by the Grand Old Man of motor racing to describe those who did not make road cars, as he did, or use their own engines, as he did. They may have bolted on the Ford Cosworth V-8 or the Renault Turbo but they still gave him a run for his money with their innovative chassis designs, and none was more of a thorn in the Commendatore's side than Dick McColl.

An immensely private man like McColl would not leave his home number, which was bound to be ex-directory, if the matter were not urgent. Alex prayed the number was correct. He dialled the last digit and heard the ring at the other end. After what seemed a lifetime, it was answered.

"McColl here." It was a crisp voice, with no trace of Scottish accent. The tone was self-assured and that of a man who knows he doesn't have to raise his voice to get those near him jumping through hoops and it reminded Alex of his colonel in 2 Para who had been only 29.

"Alex Bastyan. Returning your call. I've just got in."

"Good." McColl had not achieved his success wasting time using two words where one would do.

"I'd like you to drive for us," he said. It was more of a command than an invitation.

Alex felt his heart leap. But what a cruel business motor racing was. Johnny Abati's body was scarcely cold on some wretched mortuary slab in Dijon and his successor was being appointed. The King is dead, long live the King, he thought.

"Thank you, Dick. I accept, of course."

Any show of pleasure in the tragic circumstances would have been obscene.

"Thought you would."

McColl would have been surprised if there was a driver in the world to turn him down. Although he operated a two-car team like every other Formula One entrant, he always had a Svengali-like relationship with his number one, and all efforts were devoted to making the man of his choice world champion. Some drivers had been heard to complain, with justification, that the number two drive at McColl was like being a spare prick at a wedding. After Freddie's lax management, Alex looked forward to getting all the attention but he knew he was going to have to drive as he'd never done before.

"Are there likely to be any problems with Freddie?" McColl was asking. "Chuck Giordano's prepared to buy him off with Peterboro's mega bucks if need be."

"I don't foresee any. We've been on a gentleman's agreement since we started out," Alex said, trying not to sound too shamed.

"Good God!" McColl was astonished. "You and old Freddie were just on a handshake basis? I didn't think there were any gentlemen left in Formula One."

There's certainly one fewer now, Alex thought. To McColl, he said: "Can I just say, Dick, that I never wanted it to be this way."

"Thanks. We're all shattered. I can tell you there were times this weekend when I thought about giving up. But the sport's bigger than one man, and one team, come to that. If McColl weren't there, somebody else would. We've just got to carry on and win that third driver's championship in Johnny's memory. I'm proud that both his previous titles were won in my cars."

Alex had never heard McColl so talkative. The man was obviously more affected than he was prepared to admit.

"I can tell you," McColl continued, "that if I thought for one moment Johnny's crash had been due to a structural defect I'd've packed up for good on Friday, instead of just withdrawing our second car from the race. I'm not in the business of killing drivers."

"I know you're not. It was pure accident. One of those tragic things. That's why there's always a potential queue a mile long to drive a McColl. We all know they're built like, like –"

"Hi-tech brick shit-houses?" There was the faintest suggestion of a chuckle at the other end of the line. "I insist – and always have done – on fail-safe aircraft standards. That's my aerospace training. Every component is checked and double checked by our metallurgists and we fabricate far more than most in-house to avoid quality problems with suppliers. Things won't break on McColls while I'm around."

There was a pause and McColl continued; "There's something you ought to know, Alex, before we start working together. You were Giordano's and my first choice. We both noticed how you've never given up since the Tremayne's been way off the pace. You can take a car by the scruff of the neck and shake it. I like that in a driver. But there's one aspect I have to mention where you're sadly lacking."

Alex sighed as quietly as possible. He knew what was coming.

"You're not driving for a French-sponsored, middle-of-the grid team, you're a World Championship contender. You're with McColl now. Peterboro Chemical Corporation expects and all that. They want a bang for all the bucks they pour into us and you'll have to do your bit. That means doing all the things I know you dislike so much. It means personal appearances, press conferences, pressing the flesh, being nice to fat slobs feeding their faces in the paddock as our guests on race days when you've got a thousand and one things on your mind.

"You'll have to sign autographs till your wrist aches and be nice to the kids who are the next generation of race fans. As Chuck says, you're now a top world championship contender and it goes with the territory. He's bringing over his new top PR operator from Stateside to promote you. She goes by the unpromising name of Linda Schwerdt, I understand, but you're to give her every co-operation. She's going to make you a superstar with the media and the great British public. By the way, two million dollars for the second half of the season suit you? See you at West Drayton in the morning. You know where we are."

"There's just one last thing I'd like to get quite straight."

"Shoot," said McColl.

"The whole pit lane knows about the problems I had at

Tremayne with Thibault. Freddie couldn't control him and the little bugger seemed to think his mission in life was to demonstrate that Tremayne were running joint number ones. That way it would only be chance if I won and he didn't. God knows there's enough pressure in this game without having to put up with a team mate whose main aim in life is to give you grief. I'm simply not prepared to go through all that again."

"No problem," said McColl. "You'll find your new team mate's a real pussy cat."

Alex relaxed. "Good. That's just what I hoped. I can't imagine Johnny had any aggro from young Erwin Schrammer and I just wanted to ensure that I didn't either."

"He didn't and you won't. Everybody likes Rommel. He's the most popular guy in the team."

"Rommel? Why on earth do you call him that?"

"Because of his first name. None of us had ever heard of another German called Erwin – apart from Rommel."

"Of course! I should've twigged that. Me being an old soldier an' all. Well, he's always struck me as a nice enough young guy and I'm sure we'll get on fine."

"You will. Just think. What are Germans best at?"

"Apart from getting their towels on the beach first, I'd say.. obeying orders?"

"Got it in one! You'll be OK, Alex. We run a tight ship here."

"I know you do. That's why I'm so chuffed to be joining. Freddie's a super guy and I owe him everything but he didn't keep a firm enough grip on things. There was other – political – aggro there, due to sponsorship, I'll tell you about it some day. But I'll tell you one thing, Dick. If there *are* any problems with young Rommel I'll be the first to remind him that a chap called Alex was commander-in-chief when his lot were kicked out of North Africa in 1943!"

"There'll be no need for that. He wouldn't know what you were talking about. The poor guy wasn't born then."

"Who was? Only joking."

"I know. You'll fit in fine at McColl, Alex."

"I'm sure I shall. Just tell young Rommel that Onkel Aleksander looks forward to a suitably respectful relationship with his new nephew, Erwin. Funny how the Germans haven't done anything in Formula One for years isn't it?"

"Their time'll come round again," said McColl. "You can count on that."

The phone went dead. Alex punched the air in triumph as if he was already on the winner's podium. This called for the celebration of celebrations! The two million was twice what Freddie was paying him but he would've driven for McColl whatever sum the man had suggested. At last, he was on the championship trail and this was all that mattered.

He put the 1812 Overture on the hi-fi, turned up the volume and poured himself a rare slug of Macallan, kept for his father-in-law's occasional visits. As the music lapped over him with the warmth of the single malt, slumped in his favourite chair, he gazed round the room and tried to weigh up his new situation.

The press – or rather the meejah – should be on his side. There had been mutterings in the magazines for some time now about Britain's best driver being stuck in the doldrums unable to realise his potential. The nationals, specially the tabloids, would have a drum to beat and a British driver to root for.

Nearer home, Olivia might even wish him well in an absent-minded sort of way and welcome the fact that he was no longer with the team that contained her rival. Basically, she knew little about the way her husband earned his living. The only power she understood was provided by the horse.

Her father, Stan Heyworth, the man who had made his motor racing career possible, would be delighted. Stan would understand that a man had to renege on a gentleman's agreement made nearly a decade ago when circumstances had changed so much and a once-in-a-lifetime offer came up, however tragically. Stan would be tickled pink that his son-in-law was driving for the great Dick McColl. He would ring Stan first thing in the morning. It wouldn't be right for the old man to hear the news from anyone else.

He raised his glass as he looked round the room. Here's to you, Stan, and thanks for everything. Look where it's got us – at last. The gem of a Georgian house, set in a couple of acres, had been his father-in-law's wedding gift. Compared with the ungainly Edwardian house in Wimbledon that had been his home in the school holidays, Sutton Manor had charm and style with its high ceilings, painted panelling, and beautifully proportioned windows giving on to rolling lawns.

The house had been rundown and neglected when Stan bought it and he had spent half as much again on repairs and renovations. Olivia had then brought in an expensive firm of interior decorators. The result was in the classical Georgian mood, plenty of cream and white, reproduction period furniture and gloomy pictures of somebody else's ancestors on horseback. It was more to Olivia's taste than his and the room he felt most at home in was his study with its relaxing furniture and his trophies and books on military history.

Alex had insisted on one really comfortable out-of-character squashy armchair by the Adam fireplace and a hi-fi unit concealed in the cupboard under the bookcase next to it. Sutton Manor was home, and he was always glad to get back to it from the eternally anonymous hotel rooms of the racing season. He relished the peace and tranquillity, freedom from traffic noise and had no wish whatever to join any of his colleagues in a high rise in Monte Carlo, even if it would've saved him masses of tax. He was an Englishman through and through and the Wiltshire countryside was fine by him, although it meant extra travelling and expense.

The unaccustomed single malt was having its effect, making him feel warm and drowsy. The 1812 had given way to Tchaikovsky's First Piano Concerto. He was dozing off when he came back to reality with a sickening jolt. How the hell was he going to break the news to Freddie in the morning?

His last thought as he put out the bedside light and pulled the top sheet round his ears was: what's Caroline going to think of this treachery?

12

As he left Warminster behind on the A36 and headed eastwards for the motorway, Bracknell and West Drayton, Alex knew the time for self-doubt and introspection was over. He'd accepted Dick McColl's offer and a distinct possibility of the world championship beckoned. This was the reality, unpalatable as it might be for some. All that remained now was to break the news to Freddie in as decent a way as possible. But how? "Freddie I'm afraid I've got bad news for you," or "I'm going to have to welsh on our agreement, Freddie," or "I've had Dick McColl on the blower and he wants me to drive for him – so sorry, old boy."

How did you pull the shittiest trick on your oldest friend, whom you were already cuckolding and tell him you were about to kick him in the other ball by going to drive for the opposition? He was no nearer to working out what he was going to say and how he was going to say it when he walked up to the reception desk at Team Tremayne's modest home.

No corner of motor sport was immune from the shock waves from Dijon, especially the factory and offices of another grand prix team. Pat Russell, the plump, jolly receptionist who was normally ready for some playful badinage, greeted him gravely.

"Freddie's in conference with Mac at the moment," she said. "I'll let him know you're here. Would you like some coffee while you're waiting?"

"Thanks," he said. "Just black."

"What a terrible business about Johnny Abati. It's bad enough for the rest of us, but all you drivers must've been shattered by it?"

"I was," he said, "we all are. I should think everybody in the sport's affected. And people who've only ever seen him drive on the telly or read about him will feel a sense of loss. I should think they're flying the flags at half mast in Italy ..."

He was flipping with unseeing eyes through the back numbers of Autosport, Motor Sport and Mike Morgan's Formula One magazine, provided for visitors on the low glass table in the cramped reception area. Normally, on a visit he would go through to the workshops at the back and have a chat with the engineers and mechanics but now all he wanted to do was to get it over and get out. This time he sat in reception with a knot in the pit of his stomach feeling as unwanted as a cold-calling brush salesman.

"Freddie's free now, Alex."

"Thanks," he said, feeling anything but gratitude for what was to come.

Freddie Tremayne motioned him to the visitor's leatherette chair opposite his light oak desk. Michael Turner original paintings of Alex Bastyan in action in the blue and green team cars at Monaco, Spa and Monza lined the walls together with framed photographs of chequered flags being waved over a variety of racing cars. A glass-fronted cabinet with some trophies in need of a polish stood in the corner, topped with wilted laurel wreaths.

Incongruously, the view out of the window consisted of the warehouse of the Berkshire Carpet Company. No-one could accuse Tremayne of squandering his sponsors' substance on grandiose premises, tucked away as they were in an anonymous industrial estate on the outskirts of Bracknell.

"Dreadful weekend at Dijon, Alex. We don't want too many like that." He went on, "We don't usually see you here on a Monday. You haven't come to talk about poor Johnny Abati's accident have you?"

Thank God! Freddie had given him his opening straight away.

"I'm afraid I have - indirectly."

Tremayne looked up uncertainly.

"I don't know how to say this, Freddie. Oh hell, I'll come straight to the point. I'm going to drive for McColl," he said flatly.

Tremayne slammed his right fist down on the table. Alex had never seen him so angry. The veins stood out on his forehead and he was afraid Freddie might have some sort of seizure. As soon as he could speak, he spluttered: "You can't! We've got an agreement."

"There's nothing on paper."

"We shook hands on it. Ten years ago when we started out. I would provide the cars somehow and you would be the driver. Always."

"But that was then and this is now. Things change as you said yourself, Freddie. Of course I remember that awful day in the sleet and snow at the Oulton Park Gold Cup all those years ago when we madly decided to storm the ramparts of Formula One with an old Cooper-Maserati. How could I ever forget it? But the times they are a'changin'. You've said so yourself Freddie over things like sponsorship. What about drivers? How can you expect to keep a driver tied down for a decade? I'm 36 for Pete's sake and with all the young guys coming along I feel like a has-been.

"Hector Bonfante, Juan Baltieri, Alan Mason, Hugo Falcus – all the up-and-coming guys – are at least 10 years younger than me. We've had that one win at Monaco, which I didn't deserve, let's face it, in two seasons. Mac's lost his touch. The cars just aren't competitive any more. That's when accidents happen. When you're trying too hard, mixing it with the back markers who don't look in their mirrors.

"I'm sorry to have to say this Freddie, but I simply can't go on risking my neck in your cars. God knows I've been trying but I've been struggling for the last three seasons and thinking about a move. I haven't made any overtures to other teams. Honest. Dick McColl rang me. What could I say, feeling the way I have? You know how pissed-off I've been.

"If it hasn't been that bugger Thibault getting on my wick it's been one damn thing after another. That wheel coming off was the last sodding straw. Sloppy pit work on top of everything else. You're losing your grip, Freddie." Attacking Tremayne as a means of taking some of the heat off himself was pretty despicable but what was new?

Tremayne had been listening with growing resignation.

"I know we've been slipping," he said at last. "How can I deny it with our record? I know you feel our current car's crap but that's our lack of resources. Mac's been giving too much of his attention to a new design that's revolutionary. But we can't get it out till next season. I was really looking forward to having a car that'd give you a real chance of the title."

"Why the hell didn't you tell me that before? But it's too late now. Dick McColl's made me an offer –"

"– that you couldn't refuse!" said Freddie bitterly. "You two buggers certainly didn't waste much time. Abati gets killed on Friday afternoon and you're in the team by Sunday night."

"You've got to act fast," Alex said. "Besides, there isn't a driver who'd turn down an invitation to step into the world champion's car, even in such tragic circumstances. Try to see it from my point of view, Freddie. But how can I make you understand that I've always regarded Team Tremayne as my family? I'm sorrier than I can say for fucking you up."

"What's new when it comes to fucking up families?" said

Freddie sullenly. "Now the gloves are off, d'you think I haven't known for ages about you and Caroline? The husband's supposed to be the last to know but I knew all right. You'd be surprised at the number of people falling over themselves to tell me about you two."

It was Alex's turn to be rocked back on his heels.

"D'you mean to say you've known about us all along? Why the hell didn't you do something about it? Fire me? Have me duffed-up or whatever outraged husbands are supposed to do?"

Freddie rubbed a weary hand across his forehead. "I suppose I took no action for the sake of the team. I wanted to keep you driving my cars. But I never dreamt our agreement would involve turning a blind eye to being bloody well cuckolded. It just goes to show how we get so caught up in this business we can't see straight. We lose all our sense of values. Winning doesn't even matter. We'll do anything just to take part, just to be there. Great God! I've pimped for my own wife just to stay in the Formula One pit lane! What sort of despicable old plonker does that make me.....?" He paused but Alex knew better than to say anything.

"Of course I bloody knew. Do you think I hadn't noticed all the looks and glances when you two were in the office. And the silences at home when I picked up the phone and the mysterious wrong numbers when Caroline did. I wasn't born yesterday, you know. If there's a husband in the world who doesn't really know in his heart of hearts when his wife's having an affair, he must be thick as two short planks.

"The deceived old husband with a beautiful young wife is supposed to be a figure of fun, isn't he? There's nothing funny about it, I can tell you. You try to tell yourself you don't care. You force the pain to settle down to a dull ache. Then you accept that if pretending not to notice is the only way of keeping her – then that's the way life is."

Freddie gave a hollow laugh. "Gives a whole new meaning to the Nelson touch – seeing the signals but turning a blind eye. Of course I saw the signals. God help me, I was reduced to not letting you know that I knew.

"Take Monaco," he said with a sigh. "Do you think I hadn't noticed the way you and Caroline sneaked off? Yet with all the problems on my mind and utterly pooped as I was I had to hang around getting plastered with old Bernard for hours till it was safe to go back to the room without catching you in bed with my wife! And the night before a bloody important grand prix, too. The things I do for England and motor racing!" he said bitterly.

"You know I can still see the look of distaste on *your* face – dammit – as we met on the Casino steps. A bit rich I thought. You'd been making love to my wife and then had the bloody nerve to look all disdainful at me getting tight till it was safe to get to my own bed. You thought I was not only pissed but effusive. Too damn' right I was. Believe it or not I was glad to see you. You'd been quicker than I expected and I could get some sleep at last. I was past caring. People like me only go to bed to sleep. I've been impotent for years," he added as unemotionally as a man his age might admit to needing glasses to read small print.

Squirming with embarrassment and guilt, Alex kept his gaze fixed on the floor, anything to avoid looking his man in the eye. Freddie paused, cleared his throat and blew his nose. He then seemed to draw some comfort from the paintings of his team's occasional victories.

"Don't some people see the Formula One car as the ultimate phallic symbol?" he went on. "I suppose I did to some extent. I might not be able to drive one myself but I knew the men who did. It was almost a metaphor for my marriage. I had the power – if not much glory – of running a Formula One team. Even if I couldn't make love to my own wife.

"I've always known Caroline never fancied me sexually but she's still wonderful to live with. I knew somehow that she never enjoyed deceiving me and felt very guilty. But she always treated me with the kindness that civilised people can bring to an unsuitable marriage.

"I was prepared to settle for that and just hoped you two wouldn't last .... You know, Caroline *adorns* my life, there's no other word for it. Just by being herself and being around. I love her and I always will."

Freddie continued: "I suppose I knew something like this was inevitable sooner or later. You can't neglect a beautiful wife 18 years younger than you and hope to get away with it. An old bugger like me can't expect to keep such a lovely woman to himself for ever. In a funny way, I suppose I was almost relieved that it was you and not some young Brazilian hotshot....."

Alex winced. "That's a shitty thing to say about your own wife, Freddie. Inferring she was capable of having it off with some toyboy. I can assure you it was all my doing. Caroline was most reluctant and there was a great deal of agonising before we got really involved. I made all the running at first but now we both realise we love each other very much."

"And what about all the others you love so much? What about Olivia?"

"We all make mistakes."

Freddie snorted derisively. "And couldn't this glorious love for my wife be just one more of your mistakes? There do seem to have been quite a few over the years. Forgive me for asking."

Alex knew he deserved whatever Freddie could throw at him, but this was getting him nowhere. It was time to harden his heart and make a clean break. Off with Tremayne and on with McColl.

"I'm sorrier than I can say that it's had to end like this, Freddie. But that's Formula One. It's a rough old business."

He stood up to go and half-heartedly held out his hand. Tremayne just rotated his chair, turned his back and stared out of the window.

Alex thought he caught a glimpse of tears in the older man's eyes. Poor Freddie. Greater love, hath no man, he thought, than he layeth down his wife for his team.

13

The McColl premises at West Drayton were an eye opener; Harrods to Team Tremayne's corner shop. The comparison made Alex realise quite how remarkable was the feat of the under-funded middle-of-grid teams in winning anything.

Amazing what could be achieved when you had the fairy godmother of a huge conglomerate like the Peterboro Chemical Corporation behind you. A new clean room to lay out the composites for bodywork construction? Certainly, my dear. A workshop spick and span enough to pass a Brigade of Guards kit inspection? My pleasure. A wind tunnel, my dear? That might need an extra wave of the mega-buck magic wand but I'm sure we can manage it.

The factory was ideally situated for air freighting the team's cars from Heathrow for the far-flung races, while the transporter drivers were eagerly awaiting the completion of the much hyped M25 London ring road which should ease their route to Dover and the Continent where most of the races were held.

No sooner had Alex parked the Mercedes than Peter Foot,

the likeable chief engineer, came out to greet him with a firm handshake and a shy smile before taking him into the boardroom.

"Welcome to McColl, Alex. Dick's on the phone at the moment and asked me to welcome you. I can't think of anyone we'd rather have take Johnny's place."

"Thanks. I'm glad to be here. But not this way."

"Yes, I know," Peter said. "We're all in a state of shock, too, as you can imagine – but the fact that the show must go on helps to take our mind off things. There's so much to do getting you sorted out with the car before Hockenheim. We've got Silverstone booked for testing on Wednesday and Thursday. I know it's short notice but you'll be able to make it?"

"Try keeping me away," Alex said. "I've been waiting for years to get my hands on a McColl."

"We're all going to have to work like stink over the next week before the cars go off to Hockenheim. The wires've been humming between here and the States, I can tell you. Chuck Giordano, no less, Peterboro Chemical's head honcho, is coming over and bringing his top PR exec. I expect Dick told you that."

"Some old bird who goes by the name of Linda Schwerdt - probably a lesbian, five foot tall, five foot wide, hornrim glasses, smokes like a chimney and has a voice like a circular saw," said Alex. "I've heard all about her. She's the one who's going to make me a household name from Bognor Regis to Bogota."

"I don't know about all that," Peter Foot laughed. "But she's obviously high powered. You're getting the red carpet treatment. Chuck likes to do himself proud, Villa d'Este or the Serbelloni on Como, Hôtel de Paris in Monaco, that sort of thing. They've booked rooms at Hartwell House, a super old place near Aylesbury, set in acres of parkland. The idea is that you'll commute between there and Silverstone by chopper. It'll only be about 20 miles, so it should take a quarter of an hour door-to-door. That's you and Dick, Chuck and Miss Schwerdt. The object is to provide a comfortable relaxing aura for Miss Schwerdt to delve into your background and for Chuck to get to know you. He's a great guy. You must've seen him about in the pit lane when he's been over before from the States."

Alex nodded, "Everybody knows good old Chuck. Where would Formula One be without the Chuck Giordanos of this world? The man's a real enthusiast and he's got all that lovely money to spend. Probably thanks to him, you certainly don't do things by halves at Peterboro McColl, and I'm most impressed."

"I'll introduce you to all the guys – Dick's busy at the moment – although you'll know most of them already by sight, and then we'll get you a seat fitting."

Alex sat in the car and then had an impression taken of his back, bottom and the backs of his thighs so that the seat could be moulded to fit exactly. He was only a couple of inches taller than Abati and there was little problem in adapting the pedals. The whole thing felt so right, it was almost as if the McColl had been designed with him in mind. It wouldn't take long for it to fit like a second skin.

The grand prix driver puts on his car almost as the matador dons the suit of lights to do battle with the bulls. It has to be an extension of his very psyche with all its controls responding in the way a command impulse from the brain reaches hand or foot. But like the horseman, he senses the beast's behaviour through the seat of his pants as it transports him at up to 200 mph.

* * *

After his first few laps of Silverstone a few days later, Alex was astonished. His best time of one minute 10.88 seconds would have put him on the front row of the start for the previous month's British Grand Prix, yet this was a car he had never driven until that very morning.

He was sitting on the pit counter relaxing with a grin all over his face while smart McColl mechanics started on some adjustments to improve his comfort in the cockpit.

A tall, attractive blonde wearing tight jeans that seemed to go all the way up to her armpits, a green and white lightweight jacket and sunglasses pushed back on the top of her corn-coloured hair, came strolling down the pit lane, deep in conversation with Dick McColl and Chuck Giordano. At a distance they made an odd trio, the two men for all the world like small boys in long trousers out for a walk with teacher.

All three came up to where Alex was sitting.

"Charles Giordano you know, of course, but may I introduce Miss Linda Schwerdt?" said McColl with a rare smile. "Linda, this is the man I've been telling you about, our new driver, Alex Bastyan. Linda – Alex; Alex – Linda."

Refusing to appear as gobsmacked as he felt, Alex wiped his right palm on the chest of his overalls.

"Excuse the mitt. 'Fraid I've just got a bit hot and sweaty," he said. "How do you do?" He slipped off the counter to find that Linda Schwerdt was about half a head taller than he was.

"Nice to meet you Alex," she said with a charming smile, returning his handshake with a firm, friendly grasp. She somehow lowered one hip so that the height differential wasn't quite so great. Nice gesture, he thought, but it didn't really worry him. The old boxing adage, the bigger they are, the harder they fall, came to mind. In the old days, pre-Caroline, he'd had a taller woman than this Linda and with bigger tits. And she kept begging for more. But all that was over now that he was a reformed character.

"Nice to meet you too," he said. "So you're the one who's going to make me a household name?"

"Alex is pretty well known for his driving already," said Dick McColl. "But believe it or not, he's a shrinking violet and can't – or won't – promote himself."

"We need a bang for our bucks," said Giordano, grinning broadly and pumping Alex's hand. "When we put a lot of money into anything or anyone we sure as hell need a return. Before you know it, this good looking guy'll be opening supermarkets in Texas."

"Heaven forbid!" said Alex.

"Mr Giordano's only joking," said Linda. "Peterboro Chemical doesn't have any supermarkets, but we do have factories and we do have a lot of clients and customers we like to entertain at the races. The late Johnny Abati did us proud. He was such a lovely guy ..."

"I'm sure I'll do my best," said Alex with a sinking heart.

There's nothing for nothing in this world. You get the car, you get the chance to go for the world championship but you get six-foot blondes with libidinous legs running your life and telling the world your choice of breakfast cereal. Heigh ho. He just had to keep smiling and make the best of it. The best was undoubtedly that terrific car he'd just been driving. With that he'd have the world at his feet. Then he could surely do as he liked.

Peter Foot came up and had a few words with McColl. When he'd finished, McColl announced: "That looks like it for today. Peter tells me that the mods Alex wants in the cockpit are going to take a bit longer than he thought. We can do them in the garage and won't have to go back to West Drayton, but they'll take some time. If that's all right with you, we'll fly over to Hartwell House and should get there just in time for a late lunch. That suit everybody? Good. I'll ring the hotel and give them our earlier ETA."

* * *

Sitting in the left hand front seat of the Bell Jet Ranger, G-Susi, Alex watched his new boss make his pre-flight checks. McColl then lifted the collective, lowered the nose, turned and headed south. The headset crackled. "You ought to get one of these. It's the only way to get about in this benighted country of ours without a proper road system," said McColl.

Watching the traffic through the Perspex past his left foot crawling along the A413 to Buckingham 1,000 feet below, Alex was inclined to agree. There was probably space at Sutton Manor but Olivia, of course, wouldn't have it because it would upset her horses. If he had to keep it miles away and pay hangarage charges it would negate the whole object. Still, it was certainly worth thinking about.

"I must look into it, Dick," he said.

Over to the left the unlovely growing sprawl of Milton Keynes was visible under lowering cloud. It looked as if a front was coming in. Every time he flew at low level over the English countryside, Alex was struck by how green and pleasant much of it still was, and how little the roads stood out. The anti-road lobby constantly whingeing about the awfulness of covering Britain with concrete didn't know what they were talking about. All modern industrial nations needed a proper road network. Getting about in France and Germany was a pleasure compared with crawling on our country lanes masquerading as main roads.

In no time, the engine note had changed, the fields and woods came into sharp focus as McColl throttled back. The downdraught agitated the tree tops and rippled the surface of the lake as the machine was put down on the pad with a little shuffle like a swan settling on its nest. McColl switched everything off, set the rotor brake and the four of them stepped out into the welcome silence.

"You're right, Dick. It is the only way to travel," said Alex as they walked to the front door of the eighteenth century mansion built of honey-coloured stone.

"What a gorgeous place," said Linda.

"I kinda guessed you'd like it," said Chuck Giordano. "I always say you get the best outa folks when you treat 'em right."

"Who's the Roman-looking guy on the horse?" asked Linda as they passed the equestrian statue dominating the approach to the house.

"An earlier Prince of Wales, son of George the Second," said Alex with a flourish.

The good-natured Chuck Giordano was full of admiration. "Getta load of this guy! Not only drives race cars but knows his history. I like a fella who loves his country."

"Thanks Chuck but the Hanoverians aren't really my bag. I'm more into World War Two," Alex said airily.

"Call me Hawkeye," he whispered to a giggling Linda as they entered the house. "It was written on the base. The poor old sculptor must've twigged that no bugger would have a clue who it was in 200 years time."

An excellent lunch was interrupted by Peter Foot calling from Silverstone.

McColl returned from taking the message. "Peter says they've had a cloudburst. The circuit's awash and there's not much point in going for any more lap times. Alex did so well this morning he thinks we might as well call it a day. So let's enjoy the lunch. After the grilled turbot, Linda can grill Alex in the library over coffee."

"Gee, that's strange," said Linda. "The sun's shining here and yet it's raining like that at Silverstone."

"That's our English weather," said Alex. "It must be the most local in the world. Pissing down at one end of a tennis court, sunshine at the other and a rainbow over the net is by no means uncommon."

"I don't believe a word of it," said Linda, laughing.

"Neither do I," said Chuck Giordano.

"I'm not surprised," said McColl stolidly. "Judging from that low pressure front we saw on the way down. It's unsettled and I hope it's OK for tomorrow."

"It can rain here as much as it likes so long as we get dry races at Hockenheim, Jarama, Zandvoort, Zeltweg, Monza, Montreal and Rio," said Alex fervently. He raised the small glass of Chablis he had allowed himself in celebration. He wasn't going to admit it to Linda but driving in the wet was his Achilles heel.

* * *

"Let's start at the beginning," said Linda, clipboard ready and pen poised once they had settled into their chairs in the panelled library.

"As good a place as any," said Alex, guardedly, taking a sip of black coffee while allowing an expert eye to roam over the lightly tanned skin, wide apart blue eyes under well-formed brows, delicate nose, full soft lips and teeth that would out-sparkle any toothpaste ad. Yet she was no bimbo and an engaging personality shone through.

All this was under duress, part of the job, but he would have to go along with it. Secretly he was still hugging himself over that one minute 10.88 second lap earlier in the day. And there would obviously be plenty more where that came from.

"Please excuse my American ignorance, but there's one thing I'd like to get straight. I hear your father's a lord, so does that mean you'll be Lord Sir Alex or something one day?"

He threw back his head and roared with laughter so loudly Linda looked nonplussed. "I'm sorry Linda, that was very rude of me. Please forgive me. It's just that the idea of my being a lord is so utterly ludicrous. The only title I crave is world champion. Lords are 10 a penny. Do you know what old Monty – our general who used to get up your Ike's nose so much – used to say? He'd say 'Call me Field Marshal. There are plenty of Lords.' He was one as well, a Viscount no less.

"No, Dad's what we call a Life Peer and the title dies with

him. Sorry to disappoint you but we're not belted earls with broad acres – not like the guys who probably built a lovely old place like this. My father's a lawyer-cum-politician living in an ugly old house in Wimbledon. You know, the London suburb with the tennis courts where no male Brit has won anything since Fred Perry was in long trousers."

"A lawyer-politician?" she said. "So that means there's no history of race driving in your family?"

Alex had to suppress another guffaw at the idea of his father racing his battered old Austin Maxi. No amount of pressure could persuade Charles Bastyan to buy and drive what his son considered a suitable car, such as a new Jaguar.

"So how did you get started?"

"Very late, I'm afraid. That's why I'm one of the oldest guys on the grid. I had too many false starts at other things."

"Such as?" asked Linda.

"First, I was supposed to follow in the family tradition and read law at Cambridge. Can you imagine the sheer bloody tedium of that?"

"Bad choice. I majored in English at UCLA and enjoyed it."

"But you don't come from a family of bloody lawyers," he said.

"So what did you do?"

"I dropped out after my first year and then did a couple of years on a short service commission in the Paras. But there's no point in peace-time soldiering. It's just endless routine, doing the same things over and over again. There weren't any wars going on, apart from Northern Ireland which wasn't my idea of fun, so I got bored again."

"But how did you get started in racing?"

"By chance. It was pure chance. A brother officer and I went to a race meeting. It was only a clubbie at Brands and we watched these clowns crashing all over the place. We both thought we could do better than that. But how to prove it? We decided to take a racing school course. For me, everything clicked. I was hooked. Here was something I could really do well. It was as if all my life I'd been waiting to find myself at the wheel of a single seater - even one of those clapped-out Formula Fords the schools have to use. I didn't have much longer to do in the Army. So I said to myself, 'Right, my lad, you've got one last chance. You've flunked the law, and you're not cut out to be a peace-time soldier. This motor racing is your last chance. Third time lucky so you'd better make a go of it.'"

"It all seems to've worked out OK for you in the end," said Linda.

"Things were tough in the first year but I did get a lucky break. You'll hear the pit lane and paddock gossip that Bastyan only got where he is now because he married a millionaire's daughter to finance his start. Also, that I'm having an affair with Freddie Tremayne's wife. That's not true. It's not an affair. We're very much in love. This is just background, for your information - not for the press release."

"Of course," said Linda. "I'm only interested in your professional, not your private life," she added unconvincingly.

"As long as that's understood and I can see what you're proposing to tell the world about me before it goes out?"

She nodded.

"You're asking me about my beginnings in the sport. I don't know what it's like in the States but over here you don't get your foot off the bottom rung of the ladder if you haven't got bagfuls of your own money or sponsorship."

"It's pretty much the same everywhere, I guess," said Linda.

"My father-in-law, God bless him, made his fortune in what we call widgets, all those little nuts and bolts and brackets and grommets that every car has to have. Old Stanley Heyworth and I got on like a house on fire. I think he regarded me as the son he never had and seemed quite happy after making all that money to put some of it back in sponsoring my career in the sport he enjoyed vicariously so much. He was a frustrated racer himself but had been too busy when he was my age laying the foundations of his empire.

"Coming from a professional middle class background we weren't exactly flat broke and I was sent to expensive schools. I can't tell you what an eye opener it was to me as a 20 year old to realise quite how wealthy some of these industrial tycoons are. We were all manners and not much spare money and dear old Stan and Edna – that's my mother-in-law – were the other way round. That's as my father saw it, of course. As far as I was concerned, they were a breath of fresh air. I'd never met anybody like them.

"Stan used to bring his daughter along when he could drag her away from her horses. All he wanted to be was a sort of millionaire groupie and you'd see him at Oulton, Cadwell, Mallory, Brands, here at Silverstone, all the places where we used to race. Poor Olivia was bored rigid, and still is, hates everything to do with motor racing. My nickname was Basher Bastyan because I was crashing so often. I don't know whether he took pity on me because of that but he took a shine to me. Stan thought daughters ought to be married and as he liked me I was to be the lucky guy."

Linda, who had been listening intently and taking copious notes, interrupted him. "For God's sake! What did she have to say about that? You don't have arranged marriages in England?"

"It wasn't as blatant as that," Alex said. "I was sharing a flat with two other racing guys and I'd keep getting these invitations to go up and stay at Stan's vast mock-Gothic pile in Warwickshire – makes this place look even classier. Olivia and I would be thrown together and Stan and Edna would play cupid all the time and make arch remarks. We were both pretty young and got on well enough.

"But the contrast between all this not entirely tasteful splendour in leafy Warwickshire and the downright grottiness of three scruffy mates sharing a flat in Fulham with Y-fronts and Nomex overalls hanging on a string over the bathtub was most marked, I can tell you. OK, so I married to further my motor racing career and not for love. But I'll tell you one thing it did for me. It made me determined to stand on my own feet and make it on my own ability as soon as I'd learned my trade. I knew what the gossip was saying, of course, and that only put more lead in my pencil, stiffened my resolve. Thanks to Stan's backing, I did well enough to attract Freddie Tremayne's attention and we made it into Formula One. I've been with him ever since until Sunday night.

"The trouble is I feel I'm the biggest shit in motor racing for jumping ship and ratting on Freddie but what could I do? Nobody wanted that ghastly business at Dijon on Friday. In a strange way it's like the situation of my marriage all over again. It's a break that I don't deserve but you need all the breaks you can get in this business. How could I turn down an offer from Dick McColl? I've been hanging on by my fingertips these last three seasons with Tremayne. But with Peterboro McColl I've got a real chance of the championship."

"We'll drink to that," said Linda raising her cup. "It's been a pleasure working with you. Why did everyone warn me you were such a grouch?"

"Probably because nothing's been going right for so long," Alex grinned. "From now on Bastyan the Bastard becomes Alex the Amiable. I'm a reformed character."

14

"I've done my homework and got your racing record all documented," said Linda. "What you've just told me is kinda useful."

"I should've thought most of that stuff was off the record – and don't forget I've got the right to vet and veto," said Alex, sharply.

"I'm a professional and I do know what I'm doing. Mr Giordano thinks very highly of me," she said huffily.

"I'm sure he does. And so do I. Anything else you need to know?"

Linda blushed and smiled. "Now you mention it, I've always wanted to know what it's like to drive one of those single seaters? They always look kinda weird with those great fat tyres like doughnuts."

"I suppose they are," he said. "They're certainly no damn good for anything apart from pounding round a circuit for an hour and a half. We've come a long way since the days when people drove their cars to the track, raced 'em and then drove home again on public roads. This isn't going to be the basis of some PhD thesis on the Motivation of the Gran Pree Driver is it?"

She laughed "Of course not. I just wanna know what it's all about, that's all. There's this circus going round the world, putting on a show 16 times a year at great expense with hundreds of people involved in making the cars and runnin' the race tracks and so on. There's millions of folks watching on TV and yet only about 25 of you guys actually get to drive them. I just wanna know what it's like to sit in one and drive it. Is that so strange when it's costing us such a lotta dough?"

"Certainly not. I must try harder and give Our Sponsor due value. Are you clued-up technically?"

"No way. Eng Lit remember?"

"Nor me. Let me see, now. How can I put it in a way we can all understand? The whole object of driving one of these things is to win. As I always say, no one remembers who came second. Basically I guess it's a matter of getting all your ducks in a row. That means a reliable engine, geared just right for the circuit you're racing on; a chassis that handles like a dream; the best technical back-up from the pits, a good place on the starting grid and a clear run in the race.

"Doing all that just once is like winning the jackpot. To be world champion you've got to go on doing it and win more jackpots than 25 other guys and their teams. They're not exactly standing around feeding coins into your machine. They're pulling all their levers just as maniacally as you're pulling yours. So the guy who ends up world champion can call himself one helluva lucky chap."

"There must be more to it than luck," she said. "The guy who becomes the champ's gotta be a good driver."

"Everybody in grand prix racing's a quick driver. That's why it's called Formula One. Some are just quicker than others and have better cars, that's all. Personally, I just go flat out on all possible occasions. That way you win some but lose a lot with mechanical and other problems. That's the only way I've ever known and the fans seem to like it."

"Are you going to change now you're with us?"

"How can I? If I'm not a racer I'm nothing. Then nobody would like me. At least this way I've got some admirers. But you want to know what it's like to drive Formula One. The main difference between an F1 car and your average road car is the power-to-weight ratio. Got that? It means having a powerful engine in a very light body, lighter than our European funny cars, like the Ford Fiesta, VW Polo, or equivalent little Fiat. But it has more than twice the power of, say, a 1980 Ferrari Mondial. That means 460 horse power to propel something as light as a Fiesta. OK so far?"

Linda nodded. "I guess so. But what's it like to drive?"

"It's not comfortable, that's for sure. But you're too busy to notice that when you're strapped into this horizontal projectile like a chimpanzee in a 1960s moonshot. Hey, that's not a bad analogy though I says it as shouldn't. You're wearing all your flameproof gear because that's one thing that scares us all shitless – the idea of a fiery crash. It's amazing what the longjohns, overalls, balaclava, helmet, gloves and what not have enabled guys to survive. Your torso's strapped in tighter than a trussed turkey but you're still left with head, arm and foot and ankle movement – which is all you need, come to think of it.

"You have to be held securely so that you can withstand the acceleration, deceleration and lateral G-forces on cornering. It also helps in a shunt to be kept in the wreck rather than being thrown out and biffing the scenery. They may look flimsy but those tubs we sit in are remarkably tough and are getting stronger all the time. There's a built-in fire extinguisher system and an air supply to the helmet as well as a radio link to the pits. We've got all mod-cons, everything we need, you see.

"Flat out in sixth gear is about 200 mph, but that'll depend on the gearing for the circuit. 'So what?' I hear you cry, 'when Richard Noble has just done 630-odd in his jet car?' The big difference in our case is the constant changes of speed and direction. We've been able to corner at speeds which generate a sideways G-loading of 3.5, that's three and a half times the force of gravity.

"It's surprising how heavy the human head is – must be all that bone. Mine's about 13 pounds. Add another three and a half pounds for the weight of a crash helmet and that means a weight on the neck of over 57 pounds – if my maths is correct – in a 3.5G corner.

"It was getting absurd with feet being dragged off the pedals by the G-loads. With hard suspensions, our eyeballs were practically being shaken out of their sockets so we couldn't see properly."

"It sounds frightful," said Linda. "No wonder there's only about 25 of you guys doing it."

"It's not always like that. It's a drug, the feeling of power and control, of being on the edge. On the limit, as we say. It's that 'I am the master of my fate, I am the captain of my soul' stuff. Writ large. Who wrote that? You're the English Lit major."

"W E Henley," said Linda with a self-satisfied little smile.

"Thanks. I never could remember. Always thought it was Kipling. But it could be inscribed on our helmets and it's always stuck in my mind from school, it's so appropriate for Formula One. We all know that if we cock it up, it could be curtains. As Jackie Stewart used to say, 'When the flag drops the bullshit stops'. That's for the start. You're so busy you can go a whole race on a circuit with short straights without having time to look at the instruments. You just take in out of the corner of your eye roughly where the needles are pointing, if you're lucky. You get most of your input through your ears and the seat of your pants. I suppose it's instinct really, plus experience.

"Everything's happening at speeds that would give a traffic cop apoplexy. The trick is to slow it all down in your brain and be s-m-o-o-t-h in the way you come on and off the pedals. But the traffic's all going the same way and most of the drivers know what they're doing or they wouldn't be in Formula One."

Alex paused and looked at the ornately plastered ceiling for inspiration. "I suppose the biggest danger is at the back of the field, with guys trying too hard in the slower cars with the poorer handling. Overtaking them can be dicey at times but the experienced guy who's got some problem will always pull over and let you through. We all do that because tomorrow, it could be us in the same boat. But one thing you just don't take into consideration is the possibility of mechanical failure. If you did, you'd just never get in the car.

"You're fine tuned – at concert pitch. You can live 10 years in a 90 minute race. It's an incredible feeling. The nearer to the possibility of death you are, the more alive you are. It was a bullfighter who said it best when it comes to the ethos of extreme sports. Bullfighting was like making love to a beautiful woman when her husband comes into the room with a Browning automatic in his hand. He said his sport was the woman, the husband and the gun – all in one. I reckon most of us in Formula One would settle for that as a description.

"When you're pumped up with adrenalin like a bullfrog on LSD you imagine you're immortal. Utterly bonkers of course when your life could end in a nanosecond. But you're in such a state of ... a state of exaltation, I suppose ... that nothing matters but the moment. It would be like – like dying on the job. At the instant of orgasm. What a way to fucking go!"

His voice, which was rarely raised, carried effortlessly. Like so many Americans, Linda was fascinated by the *sound* of well-spoken English. It called to mind all those teenage hours in movie theatres swooning over Olivier as Heathcliff or Burton as Mark Antony. With his use of four-letter words in such gracious as well as public surroundings, Alex offended her sense of propriety. Linda was still the reverend's daughter even though she'd lost her virginity in high school. She could listen to Alex all day if he didn't disconcert her so much and wasn't alone in liking the singer, if not all his songs. Whatever his father might have thought of his diction, certain television and radio producers already had their eye on Alex Bastyan as a possible future commentator on the sport – with expletives deleted – when his driving days were done.

Scarcely able to believe what she had heard, a middle-aged woman taking coffee at a nearby sofa looked up sharply and muttered disapprovingly to her bald and bulky companion who shifted round awkwardly to stare. Linda smiled wanly at them, as if to indicate she shared their disapproval. Alex merely carried on without lowering the volume.

"That's what some of these young drivers seem to think – if they think at all. But then I never was a young driver. I started too late. Perhaps that's why I want to live for ever –"

He winked at the couple who glowered as disgustedly as any Tunbridge Wells residents who write letters to newspapers.

"– and have an outburst of orgasms – an ejaculatory extravaganza," he added triumphantly.

Cringing to the depths of her PR soul, Linda could only study her elegant, varnished fingernails with a nonchalance she didn't feel. Much more of this and there'd be a complaint to the management. It was dire behaviour by the client. No top American driver would be so in-your-face in public as this personable but perplexing Englishman. She could only hope that Alex would prove to be as good at driving the Peterboro McColl car as he was at alienating hotel guests. Thankfully, they couldn't be race fans or have any idea who he was.

Alex directed his most disarming smile at the couple who were now spluttering with indignation, and turned back to Linda.

"It's funny," he continued, "but there are some experiences that just can't be communicated and driving a Formula One car on the limit seems to be one of them. Drivers drive and writers write and never the twain shall meet I guess."

"What we obviously need," said Linda, delighted that the conversation was now on track, not sex, "is a Nobel literary laureate who's also a world champion."

"That'll be the day," said Alex. "But seriously, I suppose only those who've taken part in potentially life-threatening activities can know the sheer buzz of having the Grim Reaper at your elbow – although you never think of *that* at the time - and living to fight another day."

"But not everybody does. Live, I mean."

"That's true," Alex said. "You and I wouldn't be having this conversation now if Johnny Abati hadn't been killed. But you put that to the back of your mind. Human nature's a funny thing. It's always going to happen to the other guy.

"How d'ye think they got men in the First World War to climb out of a trench and walk into a hail of machine gun fire? Because every man believed *he* wouldn't be hit. His poor mates would, but he wouldn't. They used to say that the most common expression on the faces of the corpses after an attack in World War One was ...Guess what? Surprise!"

Linda shivered. "That's awful."

"I'm not trying to make your flesh creep. Formula One isn't trench warfare by a long chalk. There wouldn't be young hopefuls forming queues – lines, you say – if it were. Safety gets better all the time. D'you know the immortal Fangio, five times world champion in the fifties, said that 30 drivers died during his 10 years' racing in Europe. An average of three a year over a decade.

"It's not like that these days, thank God, largely due to people such as Jackie who campaigned so hard for safety. There are risks, of course, and we know them. We get well paid - at least in the top half of the field. Nobody makes us do it. You can't compare our lot, say, with that of a Lancaster bomber crew – or your Eighth Air Force guys in World War Two – who knew they'd be bloody lucky to survive 30 bombing missions. Or the 10,000 men of the First Airborne Division who went to Arnhem and the 2,000 who came back."

"But that was war," said Linda. "And this is Formula One."

Alex laughed. "They're both conducted with much the

same intensity. Some people would have you believe there isn't all that much difference."

"You're kidding!"

"Of course. What front-line soldier ever died super-rich? Not that all of us do. Just the luckier ones – like Johnny Abati."

15

Alex got to his feet reluctantly. Nobody had told him he'd be expected to make a speech when the idea of the dinner at the Zum Ritter Hotel in Heidelberg had been mooted. Since his second place in the world championship four seasons ago, Team Tremayne's profile had slipped and with French sponsorship, Alex had been happy to delegate any PR and speech making to his little team mate.

The army had trained him years ago in addressing syndicates, outlining plans, issuing orders and so on. That was simple enough within the structured military hierarchy. Having to stand up and ingratiate yourself with people, some of whom you hardly knew, was quite different.

The public speaking adage flashed through his mind. Stand up, speak up – and shut up. The army one: Tell 'em what you're going to tell 'em; tell 'em; then tell 'em what you've told 'em. If you can do the sincerity bit, you've got it licked, and so on. Better keep it short, he thought, and say what comes naturally.

"Mr Giordano, sorry, Chuck; Dick, Peter, all the top brass

of my new team," he looked at all of them. "Linda". He glanced to his left down the long table. "I mustn't forget the gentlemen of the press. Although when they're being rude about me –"

"Never!" shouted Mike Morgan.

"As that is so blatantly untrue I will ignore the interruption," went on Alex with a smile. "I was going to add that 'Gentlemen' is not always the first description that springs to mind."

"What's a good collective noun for pressmen?" hissed Randall.

" A pushover, or in your case, pissartist," replied Morgan. "Now belt up and let's hear what he's got to say. We don't often get the chance to hear a grand prix driver actually making a speech during the season."

"However, unaccustomed as I am to public speaking –" Alex paused for effect, "*and* to being on pole position ..." This provoked a titter and some enthusiastic applause. "I can only say how glad I am to be with a front running team. There's only one place that counts and that's first. No-one remembers who came second."

He paused for a moment. In a professional speaker it would have been a ploy to gain extra attention but Alex was collecting his thoughts.

"You know, my old grandfather had an odd expression which has always stuck in my mind. He used to say 'Life's a funny boy.' It's only as I get older that I've begun to realise what he meant. It seems to me it's this: nothing ever works out as we expect. That's for sure. All we can do is play the hand that fate deals us the best we can.

"I am most grateful for this chance and deeply conscious of the fact that it is due to no merit on my part but to the tragic loss of Gianni - Johnny - Abati, whom Italy will mourn for years to come ... He was a national hero even if he didn't drive for Ferrari. The *tifosi* took him to their hearts because they knew he would never give less than 110 per cent, whatever the circumstances. As I know to my cost.

"Whatever the conditions, he was always the master and always outdrove the rest of us. What struck me as most unfair, as an Englishman, was that he came from somewhere down south in Italy where the sun always shines – yet he was brilliant in the wet. He was unbeatable in the dry, negotiated traffic like a Milan taxi driver and always had more poles and faster laps than anyone else. He was – and is – irreplaceable.

"You don't need me to tell you that drivers were first in the queue when the egos were handed out. Everyone of us thinks he ought to be world champion, given the breaks. That's probably the triumph of hope over experience but it's probably true most years that any one of three or four drivers *could* be champion – again, given the breaks. Every few seasons, no, once in a generation there's a driver we all acknowledge as simply the best. You all know who they are: Nuvolari, Fangio, Stirling, Jimmy Clark ... You probably have your own favourites. They're just mine.

"In our day it's Johnny Abati, and I'm sure future generations will put him in the grand prix pantheon. I hope you all know me well enough to know that I'm not just saying that because I gave him a good run for his money four years ago. I just got lucky and had a bloody good car that year. My new team will be glad to know I haven't sat in anything like it until the one that got me on pole this afternoon!

"We shan't see Johnny's like again for many years. I'm glad this is a fairly low-key affair because there's nothing to celebrate."

"The old smoothie – quite the funeral oration," whispered Randall behind his hand."

"Pipe down," said Morgan. " This part can't be easy for him."

"Johnny was a great champion, and a tough but fair competitor. Nobody knows this more than I do after he pipped me to the world championship four years ago by one point. We fought toe to toe that year, slugging it out every race and I can't complain. He was the better man. Not the luckier one.

"Our ways parted after that. He won the championship again last year while I'm afraid Freddie Tremayne's team has been going through a rough patch. Johnny was the front runner while I was the nearly man. Nearly didn't finish all too often. Every race I expected to have my card marked must try harder.

"Thank God, a few perspicacious pundits – if I may call them that – were able to see I was – excuse the expression after such an excellent dinner – busting a gut, even if the points weren't coming. There can be lots of troughs in this business. And I don't mean the sort of troughs people and pigs get their snouts in. Our troughs at Tremayne have been those deep depressions you see on the weather forecast charts. And in our case they certainly seemed to be centred over our base in Bracknell, and then at whatever circuit we happened to be racing.

"Nothing succeeds like success, as the great man said. But sure as hell, nothing fails like failure. Once you get into that downward spiral it seems irreversible. Now the last thing I want to do is rubbish my old team – apart from little Banger Thibault. Everybody knows we hated each other's guts. But Freddie and I are old mates. I owe everything to him. It was only through him that I got into Formula One –"

"And his wife," whispered Randall.

"Shh!" hissed Morgan and gave his colleague a sharp kick under the table.

"But now this once-in-a-lifetime opportunity has arisen late in my career ... How could I turn it down, however badly I feel about Freddie and Team Tremayne. Life just has to go on. It's a funny boy. These things happen in motor racing. I sometimes think Formula One is a misnomer. It ought to be Formula Yo-Yo. One minute you're right up and the next you're so far down you wonder if you'll ever come up again.

"'If you don't like the heat, keep out of the kitchen', as one of your more under-rated presidents once said, Chuck. It's no good being in Formula One if you can't take the knocks."

Looking down the table to where the press were sitting, Alex raised his glass again with a smile. "Some of you *gentlemen* have been kind enough in the past to describe me – modesty forbids – as one of the, er, better drivers never to have won the championship. That goes back to Tremayne's glory days when we were able to give Peterboro McColl, Ferrari, McLaren, Lotus et al a run for their money.

"Now the wheel has turned full circle and I'm about to try to step into a great champion's racing shoes. I can only hope I'm worthy of them. This situation has occurred before, and it'll doubtless happen again, given the nature of our sport. Though it's usually a team-mate, a comrade, rather than a ... how shall I put it? ... a newcomer, who picks up the colours from the fallen leader and carries them forward into battle."

He paused, cleared his throat and went on gruffly: "Please excuse me. I'm afraid it's possible to get somewhat emotional on this subject."

There was a sympathetic murmur and nod of assent. Linda Schwerdt, whose eyes had never left him, brushed away a tear.

"But lady," he raised his glass and bowed slightly in Linda's direction, "and gentlemen, I pledge to you tonight I will do everything possible to endeavour to follow in Johnny Abati's wheeltracks."

The speech seemed to be ending on a heavier note than he intended. The last sentence came out in a rush: "I look forward to the rest of the season with my new team – we seem to've made a halfway decent start – and can only hope that what was pole today will become podium tomorrow. Thank you all, very much."

He sat down to much applause from the team and sponsors, with no-one clapping more than Linda Schwerdt. Even the cynical press applauded.

"Now that," said Mike Morgan, "strikes me as a thoroughly good, gentlemanly sort of speech. Colourful, too. I loved that bit about picking up the flag from the fallen leader. Didn't know they could be that lyrical in the Paras. Always thought they were nothing but aggression and quick reaction.

"He's a dark horse, our Alex. Getting his big break through Johnny Abati's death obviously must have got to him. It's been so unexpected. To find yourself suddenly the number one driver in the team everyone's got to beat, when you've got only nine points on the board by Hockenheim must be enough to make any driver emotional. Quite apart from the dead man's shoes element. No, I thought his speech was ace. It hit all the right notes: gracious tributes to the predecessor, humility, determination. What a change to hear a sportsman who hasn't either been robbed, rendered sick as a parrot, or projected over the moon. But I jest. Grand prix drivers aren't like that. Not the ones who can talk proper English, anyway."

"I couldn't agree more," said Randall. "But what did you expect from Alex? He *is* a gent. Public school, ex-army officer. His dad's a life peer or something."

"For Pete's sake! Did you come down with the last shower? I can see you're determined to get me on my hobby horse again. I can't vouch for the army officer class – our paths don't cross. And there've been some pretty odd life peers so that's nothing to go on. But we know all about the public schools from our personal experience of media middle management, don't we? Those berks are public school to a man, thick as two short planks – couldn't write a shopping list – and most of them are pretty shitty individuals as well. I reckon half of 'em are unemployable except, God help us, in this grey area known as 'management'.

"They get their jobs under the Old School Pals' Act and make the lives of the people who do the creative work – like us – as unpleasant as possible, slashing expenses, sending out fatuous memos and instigating petty restrictions as to who can park where.

"That is, of course, when they're not actively engaged in trying to get us sacked. Who the hell are these people to throw their weight about so much? Whoever bought a magazine, or a newspaper, because Giles Ffoliatt-Fuckin'-Snodgrass, or whoever, is in charge of admin? People buy them because they like the way we, the journalists, write. We're the people that matter, we sell the publications. Yet we're last in line when it comes to pay, conditions, and job security. If anybody's gotta go – make it a good old experienced journo.

"Then they can replace him with some lightweight kid at half the price. The fact that the mag begins to read like crap and the circulation drops doesn't seem to bother them. The stupid buggers haven't got the brains to see it's because they're sacking their best writers. They've justified their management jobs, because they've saved on the salary bill. The falling circulation is due to market forces, act of God, unfair competition – anything but their own incompetence."

Morgan raised his glass. "I give you a toast, boyo. To the damnation, frustration and final elimination of media management. Here's to hack power. Let the hand that holds the pen rule the writing roost."

Replacing his glass after a substantial swig, Morgan went on: "This ain't bad. I always used to think German reds were a bit on the Twiggy side, slender and unsubstantial, not to be compared with their more full-bodied French and Spanish cousins. It only goes to show a man should be prepared to revise his opinions from time to time.

"But I shall never change my view that being a gent in the true sense of the word, having manners and consideration for others, is innate and has nothing to do with class. It seems to come with the genes. I've known a car park attendant who's a perfect gent and clergymen who were rude sods with all the manners and Christian charity of football hooligans. No, in his funny way, I'd say Alex is a gent. I don't think anybody *but* a gent could've made that little speech. Was it straight from the heart or was it a carefully prepared impromptu?" He raised his eyes. "What a cynical old sod I am."

"I think he meant every word," said Randall. "But why is he such a, such a ... bugger for the women.?"

"Why are you such a pissartist?"

"I'm not!" Randall was indignant.

"Yes, you are! I've been watching you with that bottle of red and you've practically demolished it on your own."

"Oh, have I? Sorry. I didn't notice. Let me top up your glass with what's left." Randall changed the subject quickly. "Isn't that Linda gorgeous? She's a knockout. That slight flush, those sparkling eyes, those luscious, parted lips. Look at the way her gaze is fixed on the hero of the hour sitting opposite. She hasn't got eyes for anyone else in the room."

"Credit the girl with some intelligence," replied Morgan. "She's only just got here. She's not going to notice a bunch of grotty European press bods down this end of the table when there's the real live racing driver she's being paid to promote right opposite, now is she? I must say she looks like a gonner to me. She's showing all the symptoms of an early case of Driverdolatory."

Morgan sounded scathing. But like most people in Formula One, he relished a good gossip. And it wasn't only about which driver was going to join what team. "There's maybe already more than just a PR-and-client relationship between our Alex and the long-legged, sun-kissed Californian PR person. However, if you want my considered opinion," he went on, "I'd say the jury's out on that one."

"How do you mean?" asked Randall.

"Well, there's only circumstantial evidence and the case is not proven, as the Scots would say."

"What is it? The evidence. I'm all agog."

"You're a gog all right!" said Morgan. "Now this is only hearsay, and I may be doing Alex a grave injustice, but one has to bear in mind his previous form. Strictly *entre nous*, boyo, I was chatting to one of the Swiss journalists in the Press room today, just waiting to make a check call after phoning my national copy over. Rolf's staying in the same hotel as the Peterboro team and he was telling me all about the noises he heard in the night."

"What noises?"

"Do I have to spell it out, you prat? Bonking noises, of course. Ecstatic, female orgasmic groans and cries – in the American idiom. My old Swiss mate distinctly remembers much repetition of 'That's wunnerful, wunnerful', 'Give it to me, honey', and similar terms of endearment. In between all this trans-Atlantic appreciation was what he described as 'lusty English grunts'. It was enough to supply a tabloid headline on the lines of BRIT BEDS YANK BIRD. Is that clear enough for you?"

"Up to a point, Lord Copper," said Randall. "A grunt is a grunt, is a grunt, after all. How do you tell *English* ones?"

"How the hell should *I* know? I wasn't there. I suppose they didn't sound like German, French or Italian grunts. This Swiss guy is multi, multilingual and if he reckons they were English grunts that's good enough for me. Anyway, the couple kept him awake for what seemed hours. I know just how Rolf must've felt.

"I was once in Turin, a magnificent palazzo-type hotel – not one of your modern egg-boxes with walls as thin as a Japanese teahouse. It must've been some trick of the air-conditioning because I was kept awake by this couple having an operatic bonk in Italian and then discussing it in a most animated fashion. Funny people, Italians. When I've had my end away, all I want to do is go to sleep."

Randall laughed. "You idle Welsh windbag! Even I know that women have to have foreplay before the act and afterplay after it. They want to be cajoled, so that they can tell themselves later it was your idea, not theirs. Then they need the foreplay to get them in the mood. After the intimate and intrinsically sordid act they require after-play. Just think about it. Would you like anyone sticking their dick into *you*? Recovering from that ordeal, they need you to tell them how marvellous it was. How grateful you are and how beautiful they are when they're still all hot and sweaty. You can't just go to sleep on them. That's boring and boorish. And you wonder why you're not

Wales's gift to womanhood?"

"I've done all right, don't you worry. It's the Welsh wizardry. I'm not in Alex's class but then I'm not a grand prix driver ... You do talk a lot of rot, boyo, or you're not doin' it right. In my experience – and that of plenty of other fellers who know their Welsh onions – women actually like sex. But as I was saying before being rudely interrupted, I couldn't tell where all the noise was coming from in this grand hotel. It was as if there were secret microphones transmitting it. Most annoying, it was. There's few things worse than being forced to listen to a couple having great sex in a room near you in the middle of a sleepless night. Especially when you're on your tod.

"All this reminds me of the story of the old Scots rep who's just settling down for a wee dram in the little boarding house where he always stays near Inverness. Have you heard this one?"

"Probably," said Randall resignedly, "but go on. We've got all night."

"There he is, in his jimjams with his flask, when the landlady knocks on his door. 'Sorry to disturb you, Mr Ferguson, but this young couple has just arrived. They're on their honeymoon and I canna put them in a room with a single bed, now can I? You've got a double. Would you mind movin' next door so they can have your room? I'll knock 10 shillings off the bill,' she adds as an inducement.

"Being a decent chap, he gets his things together and goes next door. He's trying to sleep when he hears the bridegroom asking, 'Whose little ankles are those?', and the girl says 'Yours, darling'. Then it's 'Whose lovely leggies are these?', 'Whose gorgeous thighs are these?' It was driving him insane. He couldn't stand much more. Before it got to 'Whose furry little pussy is this?' he was down on his knees, hammering on the wall with his fists and yelling: 'When ye get to the whisky flask – it's mine!'"

"You can't beat the old ones," Randall smiled. "But what

your Swiss mate said is far more interesting."

"Where had I got to? Oh yes. Our friend was getting extremely pissed-off with all the sexual activity next door, like you do when you're not getting any yourself. It reached the stage where he was about to get up, thump on the wall and blow the whistle for half-time. But either he or they must've fallen asleep. He woke up later to hear a lot of whispering, giggling – you know the sort of thing – in English going on in the corridor. Then he heard what he described as a high performance car being started up and driven away – the bugger owns a new 911 himself so he knows what they sound like. Where do these muesli-munching magazine men get all their lolly from?"

"A numbered Swiss account?" ventured Randall. "He's probably got a management job on the side. He might even own the mag."

"Could be. Anyway, he heard someone driving off in something rorty. He looked at his watch and it was 3.30. He found out in the morning that Linda had the room next to his."

"Ah! But was Alex in the same hotel?"

"That's the point. He wasn't. He's staying with some German mate in his schloss. He's very popular here. They like his style, his arrogance. The question is, did he drive over in the night to Heidelberg? Who else could it have been pleasuring the newly-arrived and lovely Linda? Who else had she had time to get to know as intimately as the subject of her excellent press release? She's put out biographical stuff about Alex that I didn't know and I've followed his career closely, as you know. She must've been grilling him for hours in the motorhome after practice on Friday. A very professional lady. Highly efficient ... not, of course, that any jury would convict on the evidence. But I rest my case, m'lud, and draw your attention to the way the witness is looking at the defendant, something your lordship was good enough to point out earlier."

"Come off it, Mike," said Randall. "That's pretty flimsy. I

wish I'd never mentioned it now. The bloke in Linda's room could've been anybody who speaks – or grunts – in English. As to the way she's looking at him now, Alex hasn't exactly been ignoring her all evening. Wouldn't you make an effort, seated opposite a glorious sexpot like Miss Schwerdt? And couldn't it just be hero worship on her part?"

"And I might drive in Formula One!" Morgan laughed.

Randall took a sip of the red wine. "You should be so lucky. Of course, I've heard all the talk about Alex's love life. Isn't he supposed to have a girl at every circuit? And this torrid affair with his team owner's wife. But this business with Lindy Lou, or whatever her name is, really takes the proverbial biscuit. He can only've known her a few days. Phew! They're a different breed, these grand prix drivers – supermen on the track and superstuds in the sack – as our American friends would say."

"Good God no!" replied Morgan. "You can't judge'em all by Alex, man. He's a one-off. I reckon most of 'em live like bank clerks out of the cockpit nowadays. They have to now, there's so much more money at stake. Funny how it's all changed. Twenty years ago in Stirling's, Mike Hawthorn's and Peter Collins' day, life was far more dangerous but they seemed to have so much more fun.

"Races were often three hours or more, there was fuck-all safety either in the cars or on the circuits and bad crashes were fatal nine times out of 10. Yet the boys of that era seemed to enjoy life so much more than the present lot. They actually seemed to like each other and would share a pint after a race.

"You're too young, of course, but can you imagine an era when drivers liked to party with each other and suitable female acquaintances – not always wives? Where've the high spirits and practical jokes gone? When was the last time a grand prix driver could be seen riding round on a motorbike stark naked?

"They used to play practical jokes, silly schoolboy stunts but it meant there was an element of fun about the place. Then there was the time a driver who'd just got married returned to his hotel room with his new wife to find his mates had picked up his little hire car, carried it up a flight of stairs and left it in his bedroom. I'm only talking about the sixties – 20 years ago.

"I've never understood the point of making huge bundles of money if you can't have any fun while you're doing it. The drivers of the late fifties and sixties might be paupers compared with the present generation but I fancy they enjoyed themselves more. Perhaps adversity breeds friendship because they actually seemed to like each other's company after they'd been fighting wheel to wheel on the track for three hours without a safety feature in sight.

"What happens nowadays? After the ritual hosing down with champagne on the podium they go and skulk in their respective motorhomes. I wouldn't say Alex is exactly the life and soul of the party in the Innes Ireland tradition, but in his quiet way he's enjoyed himself, especially where the women are concerned.

"To misquote Shaw, I'd say that Formula One still provides the maximum of temptation and the maximum of opportunity for any driver who's that way inclined. The fun is probably now more on a one-to-one basis and serious instead of *en masse* and high spirited. Reflects the age we live in I suppose. When there's a lot of money at stake people have to toe the line. All except Alex who's always done his own thing.

"But if you were a good-looking boyo whose feats of derring-do were blazoned across the world's newspapers, magazines and TV screens, and gorgeous women were hurling themselves at you like lemmings headed for the nearest clifftop, what would you do?"

"If I was married," said Randall, "which he *is* – I hope I'd be able to say 'Thanks but no thanks' or words to that effect."

"Pull the other one! You pompous hypocrite. You know you'd be at it like a rat up a drainpipe. Just like the rest of us, given half a chance. But we don't get so many chances. His marriage has been a sham for ages and I don't blame him. But there's been a new Alex this year. This business with Linda is just a fling – it it's anything at all. But the affair with Caroline Tremayne is the nearest to the real thing that I've ever seen Alex involved in. Strictly between ourselves, he told me something about it. He's besotted with her and I wouldn't be surprised if there aren't a couple of divorces there eventually."

"As serious as that, eh?"

"I reckon so. You know Alex can be a pain at times but it's surprising what he'll talk to you about off the record once he knows he can trust you. You know we've always wondered why he doesn't do better in practice, particularly in tight street circuits like Monaco? He told me once that he's never had complete free movement in his right ankle since he broke it in a jump when he was in the Paras. He always feels he has to make up in racecraft and sheer aggression on Sundays what he lacks on Fridays and Saturdays.

"What I like about Alex is his honesty. He won't bullshit you. If he's made a mistake he'll say so, instead of trying to blame the car. If the car's going badly he'll get incandescent. He doesn't seem to care what's quoted. No wonder he's had trouble with the sponsors. If he thinks something's rubbish, he'll rubbish it."

"You're lucky, Mike. I don't know him as well as you do. I've always reckoned he was never going to win the pit lane's Mr Nice Guy contest. I should think they hate his guts in Tremayne for leaving them in the lurch. To be screwing the boss's wife only adds insult to injury. Wasn't there a great hoo-ha as well at Spa about one of the mechanics getting sacked after a wheel came off?"

"I know," said Morgan. "Alex told me he was sorry about that. It was just heat of the moment stuff. Think how hyped up he must have been, slamming into the Armco. Just imagine it, the car falling to bits all round you in a huge shunt.

"He didn't expect Freddie Tremayne to sack the guy. He was just letting off steam. Everybody overreacted. Don't forget team morale was low at Spa. Alex's win at Monaco was the only success they'd had for ever, apart from Banger Thibault picking up a couple of sixths. Freddie made no allowance for Alex's state of mind. Hell, man, he'd just escaped death by a whisker. Tremayne blew his top and told this chap Stevens he'd better clear off.

"Instead of waiting for things to calm down, Stevens did just that. There and then. Apparently he thumbed a lift out of the circuit and phoned Freddie for his P45 on the Monday. The guy was obviously determined to make a martyr out of himself – a bit unbalanced I'd say. There's often more than one side to any story but if Alex is in the frame anywhere he's the one who gets the flak. He's just that sort of chap. Controversial's the word."

"I didn't realise that," said Randall. "Perhaps he's more sinned against than sinning?"

"I wouldn't go so far as to say *that*," replied Morgan with a smile. "He's a sinner all right. Aren't we all? Did I ever tell you my dad was a chapel lay preacher? I was brought up on sin and the avoidance thereof. We didn't even have a telly in the house in case we kids were corrupted.

"Dear old Da, just as well he didn't live to see the way I've turned out. He was knocked off his bike and killed by some rich kid showing off to a girl in his dad's Jag. I guess that's when I stopped believing. How can you ... when a lovely man pedals through the night in the pouring rain to preach the word of God at a tin tabernacle in the valleys and gets wiped out for his pains?

"It destroyed our Mam. She's never been the same since. He was only the age I am now – early forties – and all Da ever wanted to do was sell lots of tickets for British Rail at the station during the day and preach in the evenings and at weekends ... sorry. All this excellent wine is making me maudlin.

"Good God! Do you realise what the time is? The waiters are hovering to lay the places for breakfast and everybody's buggered off. All our mates down this end of the table went ages ago; Eric's gone and good 'ole Randy Barnett, everybody's favourite Yank; Pat and Big Benny, Dino and Jacket, Eoin and Maurice, Alan and Nigel. Funny how we seem to hunt in pairs - and I'm stuck with you ... Still, we'd better say thanks to our beautiful hostess, make our excuses and scarper. That leaves only Alex still chatting up Linda. You'd never think the man had a motor race tomorrow."

* * *

"To my mind that proves it," said Randall as they were driving in the battered little VW hire car back to their hotel.

"Proves what? Don't speak in riddles, man," said Morgan irritably. "It's tiring enough trying to keep this heap on the road as it is."

"That Alex isn't bonking Linda. The fact that they were just sitting there chatting so late. The only people who do that are old married couples not so bothered about sex or those whose interest in each other is purely platonic. In my limited experience, people at the start of a red hot love affair are at it – to use your descriptive expression – like rats up a drainpipe. If your theory were correct they would have left discreetly and separately ages ago and should, as we speak, be making the beast with two backs and the bedsprings twang like guitars."

"Very poetic, boyo," Morgan laughed. "I'm supposed to be the Welsh wizard with words – and women. I fear we may never know the answer to that delicious little bit of scandal. But I'll tell you one thing: we're going to be a lot busier in the second half of this season. Johnny Abati was a great driver, though I'm not sure he's quite as great as Alex made out. Time alone will tell but he was Italian, after all, which means he didn't count for half as much in Fleet Street as he did in his native land.

"Every time I get on the phone with my tabloid stuff, the copy-taker groans: 'Ain't you got no geezers wiv English names?' I have to explain to him as gently as I can that Brits aren't winning anything much these days. But that could change literally overnight. Now Alex's got Abati's seat we're going to be chronicling his bid for the title, boyo.

"And it's such a long time since we've had good news stories about a British driver. I'm really looking forward to it. Pity he's English. We've had the Scots. Why can't we ever have a potential Welsh world champion?"

"Perhaps because Welshmen drive the way they play rugby?"

"You bugger! You've only got the guts to say that because you know I've got my hands full of steering wheel. I'll deal with you later. But mark my words. We'll be getting a new hero on our hands. I can see the headlines in the old Muckraker above my mutilated little stories. Instead of BAD BOY BASTYAN it's going to be BASTYAN MONARCH OF MONZA, etcetera, etcetera."

"With any luck," said Randall.

"Of course. They all need all the luck in the world. The race tomorrow will be a scorcher. Hockenheim always is. I can't get away with it in the mag but in my tabloid pieces I refer to it as The Cauldron. I thought of the Coliseum originally but that's too many syllables and they'd probably think the race was down St Martin's Lane and round Trafalgar Square. Heigh ho, when all's said and done, it's nice to have the staid old columns of the mag to fall back on. At least you don't get the daft mistakes due to telephone mis-hearings. I've had drivers retiring at 'half-pistons' instead of half-distance. I've reported on that wonderful new woman driver Maria Andretti and had 'star-lit' instead of scarlet Ferraris under my by-line."

"You can't win 'em all," said Randall sympathetically. No-one had invited him to supplement his income sending grand prix reports to a national newspaper.

The red wine and the little car's motion had their effect and he nodded off as Morgan drove them back to their hotel thirty kilometres away.

"It couldn't have been Chuck Giordano," the Welshman said suddenly. "He'd grunt in Italian-American. Why couldn't it have been Dick McColl?"

"Eh, what doing?" Randall woke up with a start.

"Loving the luscious Linda, of course."

"We're back to that again, are we? I thought Dick McColl was just in love with Formula One. Isn't he?"

"Aren't we all? But that doesn't provide sexual relief. The man's a bloody little genius but he's human and presumably gets the urges that torment us all. Let's face it, Linda is remarkably urgeworthy. She certainly gets my libido looping the loop."

"Sorry Mike. I can't buy that. She's got to be at least a head taller than he is."

"So what boyo? Tall girls learn to be philosophical. To them we're all the same length lying down. And don't forget the aphrodisiac of money, power and fame. I reckon Scott Fitzgerald and Hemingway were wrong about the rich being different because they had more money. I maintain the rich are different because they can have any beautiful woman they fancy – even if they do look like Frankenstein's monster. Not that McColl's ugly. He's unremarkable to look at, *ordinaire*."

"Just like most of us," said Randall.

"Speak for yourself, boyo."

"Alex Bastyan isn't ordinary."

"Interesting you should say that. I've known him 10 years so I don't really *see* him at all. They used to say no man was a hero to his valet and he sure as hell isn't to a cynical old journo. Tell me, Pete, how you see Alex Bastyan? Describe the man to me. Use your writer's flair, boyo."

"Let me think now," said Randall, trying to collect his tired and befuddled wits. How he wished he had the Welsh Windbag's mental energy and ability at that time in the morning after a day's work and a big dinner. He was learning that stamina was a prerequisite for grand prix coverage. "Well, he's not tall, about five foot nine, I'd say. Slim but muscular. Immensely fit – looks as though he could run a four-minute mile and then climb the north face of the Eiger and not get out of breath."

"You can do better than that. They all have to be fit to withstand the G-forces and not get tired. What about his persona, his appearance, his looks, the image he projects?"

"I'd say he's not conventionally good looking in the way of having handsome features or anything. But you can see why the birds fall out of the trees for him. It's that direct, challenging way he has of looking at you. Those grey-green eyes seem to bore into the back of your brain. It's his arrogant, 'I don't give a damn about you until you've proved you're worth my attention', sort of attitude that would reduce most women to jelly. I can see that. As to his actual looks, he's got a firm jaw and interesting lines on his face. Women like that. His overall aura is ... well, I'd say it's somehow disturbing. You're always aware of his presence even though he's not a big man physically. I'd say he's got charisma in spades."

"Not bad at all, boyo. You're beginning to use your eyes, to notice things and that's an essential part of the reporter's stock in trade. Because if you don't take in what you see, how can you report it to your readers? I'd say you've got our Alex quite well sussed. Still it's hardly surprising that this predator who's had more women than you've had hot dinners seems to've been tamed at last by Freddie Tremayne's wife ..."

"I don't think I've seen her. What's she like?"

"You'd know if you had. Once seen never forgotten, but she hasn't been around much lately although she used to come to all the races. What's she like? Absolutely gorgeous. There are no other words to describe her. You're an old black-and-white film buff – the best way I can define her physically is a cross between Hedy Lamarr for the fine, exotic beauty; as to the figure, well that's got to be Marilyn but without the overtness, and the ladylike aura is Princess Grace. Underneath it all I'm sure she's a complete sex bomb. It's a very potent combination, and it's got our Alex completely besotted. I've always found her charming, intelligent and perfectly pleasant. But it's difficult to keep your mind on the conversation because it tends to stray down erotic paths. She's that sort of woman. She's only got to cross those wonderful legs for my sap to start rising ... Anyway, here we are. The Hotel Bad*schlafen*. Uncle Mike has delivered you to your door safe and sound yet again. Let's hope Alex gets a good night – wherever he's sleeping – and wins tomorrow."

"Amen to that," said Randall.

16

On hands and knees in her old gardening clothes and a scarf round her head, Caroline Tremayne winkled a dandelion with a four-inch root out of the paving by the front door of Hambledon House.

As she tossed it into the wheelbarrow, straightened her back with a grimace and looked at her watch yet again, she felt a sudden pressure and warmth on the back of her neck and shoulders.

"You've left it a bit too late this time, old chap," she said. "I'm just going indoors. It's nearly time for the race report." Oscar, her black cat with the white shirt front, answered with a contented purr as she reached back and rubbed his cheek. "Now what have you been up to? Not trying to catch those fledgling robins, I hope. You've been ticked off about that before. And I wish you wouldn't keep bringing those dear little field mice in and losing them behind the panelling ..."

The soft fur was warm against her skin and slightly perfumed. "No. I should think you've been snoozing in the sun by the lavender bushes and only just noticed I was doing all this damn weeding. Hold on! I'm going to stand up."

Rocking gently back on her kneeling pad, she got to her feet. Oscar scarcely moved and didn't even need to grip with his claws. It was all done by balance. Gently holding the cat's tail which was twitching by her throat, Caroline walked through the cool, stone-flagged hallway to the low-beamed kitchen at the back of the comfortable old house, dominated by the cream Aga in the big fireplace.

Relishing his role as living fur stole, Oscar stayed put as she removed her gardening gloves, changed the water in a vase of roses on the window ledge, poured herself a glass of Amontillado, turned on the radio, permanently tuned to Radio Four, and sat down at the kitchen table.

"The German Grand Prix at Hockenheim today was won at record speed by Alex Bastyan of Britain in a McColl-Renault ..." said Simon Taylor.

Caroline gave a spontaneous cry of joy and clapped her hands, startling Oscar. The cat stepped off her shoulders on to the table and sat down, wrapping his tail about him and ostentatiously turning his back to show displeasure.

"Sorry, Oz, but it's such wonderful news," she said, absent-mindedly stroking him as she listened.

"Bastyan," the report continued, "led from start to finish. This was an incredible performance as he has only just joined the team, taking over from the world champion, Johnny Abati, who was so tragically killed in a freak accident in practice at the French Grand Prix a fortnight ago.

"Finishing second, some ten seconds behind was Guy Antoniazzi of Italy in his Ferrari V-12, while helping to make it a great day for British motor racing, Alan Mason was third in the Lotus-Ford.

"Run in heatwave conditions, the ultra-fast Hockenheim track took its usual mechanical toll and there were only five cars on the same lap at the finish. But Hockenheim this year belonged to Alex Bastyan who turned in a bravura performance with a car he sat in for the first time only last week. Even his rushed testing programme at Silverstone before the transporter had to leave to bring the team cars to Hockenheim was cut short by rain.

"That makes his ability to dominate practice and take pole position at a speed of over 141.5mph all the more impressive. He also set the fastest lap in the race at 136.3mph and won at an average speed of 132.4mph for the one hour 25 minute 56 second race.

"The last few seasons have been frustrating for Bastyan, often described as Britain's leading driver. The Tremayne-Ford team has sadly been unable to provide cars to match his talent but now he is with one of the front-running teams he has shown just what he can do ..."

Caroline winced. "It's true, Oz. Our cars have been a bit off the pace."

" ... after Dino Morandini dropped out with a blown engine in his Ferrari at half-distance there was no-one to give Bastyan a run for his money in the flying McColl. It was a great day for Britain because not only does Bastyan seem to have set his foot at last on the world championship trail, but because Alan Mason was also on the podium.

"The Argentinian, Hector Bonfante, was fourth in his McLaren-Ford, while Hugo Falcus of Belgium was fifth in a Tyrrell and Pedro Jalapeno of Brazil sixth in a Lotus.

"After eight rounds, the late Johnny Abati leads the world championship with 28 points although his total will now be overtaken. Bonfante has 25 points, followed by Antoniazzi with 23 and Bastyan with 18. Now that Alex Bastyan is in a truly competitive car, wearing the mantle of that great champion Johnny Abati, the fight for the world championship is well and truly joined. Simon Taylor, Hockenheim."

"Thank you, Simon," said Caroline, switching off her set. No other sport had ever really interested her apart from hockey and that rarely seemed to be reported on either television or radio.

Poor Freddie. There had been no mention of the Tremaynes

which presumably meant they had perished early in the race. Much to his delight, little Teo-Nicolas was now team leader and had been joined by another Frenchman with a funny name, Pete Jankowski. If the team hadn't been having much success with Alex, what hope was there for it with those two? Jankowski was supposed to be good, having won the European Formula Two championship ...

Scooping up Oscar in her arms she went through to the sitting room and sat him down at the desk in the corner. Freddie had his study but this was where she did the household accounts, paid the bills and wrote letters.

Getting her notepaper out of the drawer, she picked up her fountain pen, entered the date, wrote 'My darling Alex' and then paused. Oscar put out a playful paw and sparred with her pen. She chided him gently.

She didn't know what to write. There had been no contact since May and it was now mid-August. Alex had joined McColl and she couldn't blame him. The man was a professional racing driver and many thought he deserved to be world champion. He had stayed loyally with the team for years which probably meant he had turned down offers from elsewhere, although they had never discussed it. She really couldn't find it in her heart to blame him, although Freddie had called him 'a bloody Judas for taking McColl's 30 million pieces of silver.' Caroline sometimes wondered what her husband regarded as the greater perfidy, Alex's adultery with her or the defection to McColl.

She was still living in what the lawyers called 'the marital home'. Hambledon House was a lovely old place and she was very fond of it. Freddie had said nothing as yet but she would obviously have to move out. The dear man had not even mentioned divorce but that was surely inevitable.

Bored with the lack of attention, Oscar moved six inches and sat down on her writing paper, pushing his head up under Caroline's chin.

"Don't sit there, Oz, or you'll get ink on your bottom," she said. "Still, I suppose it won't show on you, although you wouldn't like the taste of it next time you gave yourself a wash."

She thought of Alex. Some men seemed to be nothing but overgrown small boys who entwined themselves around your heartstrings. *My true-love hath my heart and I have his/ By just exchange and one for the other given/ I hold his dear, and mine he cannot miss/ There never was a better bargain driven*, were the only lines she could remember from school, written by that gorgeous man Sir Philip Sidney, the ultimate romantic figure for a literate schoolgirl crush. She had Alex's heart but there had been no pledge, no agreement made, no declarations of undying love. The bloody man was always too damn busy driving racing cars.

There'd been little more than an ecstatic exchange of bodily fluids whenever the opportunity presented itself. What basis was that for a lifetime of bliss when the wells of their wonderful lust ran dry?

Alex was like a tiger with its freedom. He could express himself in the cockpit of a Formula One car. What would he be like deprived of that outlet for all his pent-up aggression, that killer instinct that was going to make him a world champion? Somehow she knew that under all that macho armour with which he kept the world at bay, she had his heart.

The legendary womanising everybody warned her about counted for nothing as far as she was concerned. Sex without love was simply relieving an itch. She and Alex knew what real love-making was. What man worth knowing didn't have some devil deep inside him that drove him to excess? What was ever achieved by moderation in anything? That was the trouble with dear old Freddie, he was simply too nice ... Which was why she loved him still but not in the way she loved Alex. She *adored* him.

It couldn't just be the sex. Or was the sex so wonderful because of what she felt for him? Caroline had had remarkably little sexual experience before her wedding and not a great deal after it. Until she met Alex.

But what could she write to this man who overwhelmed her? Should she write to him at all? How could she express what she felt? She was no Philip Sidney. She hoped Alex would understand why she was keeping away from the grands prix. That slap in the Hermitage at Monte Carlo had taught her that nothing and no-one came between a Formula One driver and his goal. She knew instinctively that he would be devoting himself one hundred per cent to trying to win the world championship with McColl. No man could do it on his own. It was a team effort, as she knew only too well after all Team Tremayne's barren years.

But what better combination than Dick McColl's genius, Peterboro Chemical's millions and Alex's ability? He had tried so hard for so long, getting so desperately bad tempered and frustrated with Tremayne's lack of competitiveness. Alex once told her the only solace he could get was between the breasts of the first beddable beauty to present herself.

He would have no time for women now. Not even her. But she would go to him once the season was over. She wouldn't even distract him with a letter. He would somehow know he had her heart – whenever he had time to give it a thought!

"C'mon Oscar, up you get. Alex is going to have to get along without a letter from us after all. Even if we sent one he wouldn't have time to read it."

Caroline sighed, screwed up the sheet of paper and dropped it into the wastepaper basket. Picking up the cat and placing him over her left shoulder she walked into the garden still bathed in the soft sunlight of a glorious summer evening.

"Dear sweet Oz," she murmured. "What would I do without you, with the man in my life so far away? Just as well we're on our own and nobody to hear you and me having all these one-sided conversations. Is this what's to become of me – a lonely woman with no-one but her black cat to talk to?"

17

Alex had to concentrate hard on technical discussions at West Drayton. With Jim MacGregor in the early days at Tremayne he had enjoyed a mystical meeting of minds. He had only to feel something about the car for Jim to be able to divine his thoughts and translate them into castor angles, spring adjustments, wing settings and so on.

He didn't delude himself. It was not on the same level of magic as the rapport between Jimmy Clark and Colin Chapman and the great days of the 1960s when Lotus ate the opposition for breakfast. On their scale of 10, he was about 3.5. For the last couple of seasons at Tremayne, Big Mac seemed to have lost his touch and however much time was spent in technical discussion the result on the track was disappointing.

With his new team, McColl, it was like being back at school. Peter Foot and Dick McColl were on a different plane and less sympathetic with his lack of technical eloquence and fluency. He shuddered to think what might happen if they produced a car he couldn't handle.

He was paying close attention during his meeting with McColl and Foot before the Italian Grand Prix when the phone rang.

"Fuck!" said McColl. "I told Kim we weren't to be disturbed." Still frowning, he passed the receiver across his desk to Alex.

"It's for you. The missus. Says it's very urgent."

With his hand over the mouthpiece, Alex said: "Sorry, Dick. I can't imagine what she wants – she never once phoned me at Tremayne." To Olivia he snapped: "I suppose you realise you're interrupting an important conference."

"It can't be more important than Daddy's life," she said bitterly.

"What's that supposed to mean?"

"Just that he's had a heart attack! He was at home, thank God. Ma got him to Leamington Hospital in 20 minutes but they don't give him much of a chance. It was a massive one. I'm ringing from the hospital now."

"God!" he said. "Poor Stan. How awful."

Looking across to Dick and Peter, he said: "It's Stan Heyworth, my father-in-law. Olivia says he's had a heart attack."

"I *am* sorry," said McColl, getting up from his high-backed, swivel chair. "Peter and I'll be in the workshop. Take your time."

Alex nodded his thanks and listened again to Olivia.

"As soon as he could speak the first thing he wanted to know was where you were. 'Why isn't Alex here?' he kept saying. You must drop everything and get up here straight away."

"You know I can't do that, Olivia. Stan wouldn't expect it. He knows what's at stake. We've got some important new mods on the car that I'm being briefed on. We haven't even had time for testing as the transporter's on the way there. Tell you what I'll do. I'll get the first plane out of Linate after the race on Sunday. We'll arrange a chopper out of the Autodromo as soon as the race is over. Sooner, if I don't finish. I'll be in Leamington on Sunday night, you'll see."

"You bastard!" He winced and held the phone away from his ear. "You owe everything to him. He's dying and yet you won't even come to see him. You claim to love him so much. What sort of a man are you?"

"I've told you. I'll be in Leamington on Sunday night."

"He could be dead by then." Her voice was emotionless.

"C'mon, Olivia. You always exaggerate. He's tough as old boots and'll outlive us all. For Chrissakes, I've always loved Stan like my own father. There are times when I wonder whether *my* father's on the same planet. Stan appreciates what motor racing's all about. He knows I can't *not* go to the Italian Grand Prix, even if I wanted to. Give him my love. Tell him to watch it on the box. That I'll try to win the race just for him – I'll dedicate it to him. I'll see him on Sunday. 'Bye Olivia and try not to worry too much. He'll be OK."

Putting the phone down, Alex was in no mood to be yelled at by an overwrought wife, even at long range. The news about Pa-in-law was bad enough in itself. Stan was always like an overgrown small boy with his bubbling enthusiasms. Indestructible and nothing like 58 or whatever. Why should he, of all people, be struck down?

He wasn't overweight and always said he'd never had the time to be ill. He'd worked like a dog to build up HMG – the Heyworth Manufacturing Group – starting from a workshop in a back street in Balsall Heath and deserved the millions he'd made.

Now, when he was at last able to ease up a bit and have more time to relax and enjoy his beloved motor racing, this had to happen. It was so bloody unfair. Stan was one of life's enhancers and seemed to have achieved his business success without making enemies. You never met anyone who had a bad word to say about him.

There were people who had worked at Heyworth's for 30 years yet it was no deadbeat organisation rooted in the past.

Stan's enthusiasm kept things fizzing and he had design and production men scouring the world, and Japan in particular, for new methods and ideas to make sure his products were always competitive. "Even if you're only making widgets, they might as well be the best produced widgets in the world. Otherwise, sure as God made nuts and bolts, a little bugger in Taiwan – or somewhere – will undercut you on price and quality," he used to say.

Deep down, Alex didn't feel nearly as confident as he'd just pretended for Olivia's benefit over the phone. He realised she would never have rung up unless Stan's condition was serious.

He went in search of Dick McColl's secretary. It would be Kim's task to organise the travel arrangements now needed to get him from Monza to Leamington as soon as possible after the race on Sunday. He thought a scheduled jet with helicopters at both ends would probably be quickest but that wasn't his problem.

His job was to make sure he knew how to get the most out of the latest car as soon as the team transporter delivered it to the historic Autodromo Nazionale di Monza for the first practice session on Friday. He had to *concentrate*.

* * *

Still clutching the huge florid silver trophy awarded to the winner of the Gran Premio d'Italia, Alex pounded up the stairs of the Leamington Hospital. He paused for a moment to steady himself outside the ward door before going in.

Olivia and her mother were weeping without a sound at each side of the bed. One look told him he was too late.

"I've brought him this," was all he could say, proffering

the cup.

Edna scarcely noticed but Olivia reacted immediately. Dabbing her eyes, she gave him a withering look. "A fat lot of good that is. So you won again. That must make you very happy. What Daddy wanted was you - not a bloody trophy."

"For God's sake, Olivia," he said in a hushed whisper. "Do we have to row over Stan's deathbed? I did my damnedest to get here. When did he – "

"Die? Half an hour ago. It's the end for all of us. Daddy's gone now and you can go out of my life too. There's no reason for you to stay, is there? I've always known you only stayed married to me because you felt you owed a debt to him. Well, he's released you now."

She spoke quite rationally. Her voice was level and calm while her mother sat motionless, staring at nothing. Drained and empty as he was, the contrast between the near hysteria of the Monza crowds he had left and the two mourning women by the bedside in the little white room was all the more poignant.

More than a life had ended. In her matter-of-fact way Olivia had made that quite clear. She was Stanley's daughter all right. How strange it was that he had never been able to get on better with the daughter of the man who meant more to him than his own father.

He knew it was all over but there was still something to be done. Placing the trophy on the bedside locker, he said: "I know I don't deserve anything of the Heyworth family. But will you do one last thing for me? Put this in the coffin with him? Stan would've liked that."

Olivia's lids might have been red from crying but the look in her grey eyes was as flinty as he had ever known it. Suddenly, she relented.

"If that's what you want? Of course. But don't you need it for the trophy room? You've waited a long time to win Monza."

He shrugged. "I dedicated the win to Stan. It's his." Glancing helplessly at Edna, he turned back to Olivia. "I'll move out of Sutton Manor immediately."

"Where will you be? You'd better leave a forwarding address."

Typical Olivia, practical as ever, even in the twin crises of her father's death and the break-up of her marriage.

"I'll probably move into a local hotel until the end of the season," Alex said. "I haven't got time for househunting. Would you mind re-directing my mail to the factory in the meantime? I can always pick it up from there. I'll send for my things as soon as I'm settled. Is it OK to leave them till then?"

"You'll get your mail at West Drayton – I'll see to that," Olivia said matter-of-factly.

She didn't hate Alex. She had no desire to hurt or try to humiliate him. At one time, she had been exasperated beyond endurance by his infidelities until she learned to realise that they didn't really mean anything. They were due to his loveless upbringing and a sexual exuberance that he ought to have outgrown years ago.

As men couldn't be gelded like over-frisky horses, perhaps she ought to have been putting some libido depressant in his tea. Not that he was ever at home to drink it. She supposed that it was his incredible vitality and virility that made him the driver – and the man – he was. Otherwise, he'd be a shorn Samson.

The English boarding school system had a lot to answer for. Creating sex-starved late developers – or poofs. Alex was certainly no poof. But his affair with Caroline Tremayne was different. At last, here was a woman who could probably sort him out. For all their sakes, Olivia hoped something could be worked out, although poor old Freddie never featured in the equation...

She knew her occasional presence at races had been resented but it was only about once a year and mainly because her parents thought her perpetual absence odd. Now her father had gone everything had changed. There was no point in trying to hold on to a man who didn't want you. She was just thankful the marriage had at least lasted her father's lifetime and he had not lived to see its end.

Pa had loved Alex so much and it had been mutual. She couldn't *hate* Alex. She now just wanted to live her own life. The sex he used to get so excited about in the early days of their marriage had never meant anything to her. How could you miss something you'd never enjoyed in the first place? Who needed a man anyway when she had just lost the only one she ever really cared about?

Looking up at Alex standing downcast by the bed, she said: "You surely don't imagine I'm going to put your things in the barn for rats to chew on or just dump them on the drive? Just let me know a week or two in advance when your removal men'll be round. You know how busy I am with the horses."

"Thanks. I'll do that."

He could no longer bear to be cold-bloodedly discussing footling domestic arrangements in the hospital where the man he loved best in the world was lying dead. He had to get out. The atmosphere of reproach was almost tangible. Whatever Stan's widow and daughter were thinking of him, it could not match the burden of regret he would carry.

Apart from the irreplaceable Stanley it was the end of his marriage. Time for the legal vultures to tear at the carcase. How right he'd been not to get stuck into the law all those years ago. Fancy making your living out of other people's misfortune. At least Formula One didn't do that, even if it did mean you couldn't grant a dying man's last wish.

"I'm sorrier than I can say that it's had to end like this, Olivia."

Why did he have to keep saying that? Wasn't that what he'd said to Freddie Tremayne? All his personal relationships were a disaster area. And now he'd lost dear old Stan, the man who'd made his racing career possible. Why couldn't the old boy've been spared to see him winning the world championship? Fifty one points on the board and three races to come. Another win in Canada in a fortnight's time and with any luck, a leader board spot in Brazil would be enough to do it, without even bothering about the last race in Japan. Stan would've been even more delighted than he would....

Engulfed in his distress, he was scarcely aware Olivia was speaking to him.

"I'm sorry too, Alex."

She spoke with an unfamiliar tenderness. She surprised him even more by holding out her left hand in a gesture not of reconciliation but of ruefulness and farewell. He touched it briefly.

Edna looked up at him across her husband's body. He lipread rather than heard her say, "Good bye, Alex."

18

Dick McColl punched the Brazilian air in triumph as the green and white car flashed over the line. The constructors' championship was his and Alex had won the world drivers' championship. In a rare moment of emotion he turned and hugged Peter Foot, an embrace rendered less intimate by a clash of the headsets they both wore. The rest of the McColl team members were jumping up and down, shouting, cheering and slapping each other on the back.

Everyone knew that Alex was not one of those who drove canny races for a few points rather than striving all out for victory. This time he had had problems and a pit stop but he had come back through the field in a storming finish to be third, capturing four points to clinch the championship.

The Brazilian race fans were delighted with the victory of their own man Hector Bonfante but they were good natured enough to hail Alex as the new champion on his slowing-down lap. The crowds cheered, the marshals waved their flags, samba bands in the stands tried to make themselves heard above the general outpouring of Latin-American enjoyment.

It was carnival all over again except there were Formula One cars instead of floats and only the helmeted heads of men to see rather than the bodies of beautiful women.

The more emotional drivers have been known to shed tears of joy on winning their first grand prix, let alone the world championship. Alex felt a fierce exultation, mixed with a sense of unreality and exhaustion. The acceptance that he was world champion would sink in later. Motor racing has nothing more to offer than this moment, he thought, as he threaded the car through the throng swarming all over the pit lane.

"Well done, Alex! Well done! Stu-fucking-pendous!" The usually monosyllabic McColl shouted to make himself heard above the clamour as Alex climbed from the cockpit, removed his helmet and sweat-soaked balaclava.

Bastyan and McColl pushed their way through the journalists, cameramen, photographers, pretty girls and other well-heeled hangers-on who find their way into pit lanes round the world, despite the rigorous pass system.

At the back of the garage which was at least out of the fierce sun but little cooler, Alex drank deeply and doused himself with water.

"I've got something for you," said McColl. Alex recognised the writing on the unstamped bulky envelope. Instead of stuffing it into his overalls pocket he started to slit it open with a sweaty thumb.

"There's no time for that. Read it later," said McColl.

"For God's sake, Dick! It's from the woman I love."

McColl was about to say 'which one?' but thought better of it. Alex would know that he knew the letter was from Caroline Tremayne. Poor woman.

"Just leave me alone, for a mo," said Alex peeling back the top half of his overalls to try to get some relief from the overpowering heat and sitting down on a tool box.

"Pull yourself together, man! You're the new world champion. The world's press is waiting to talk to you and there's a press conference to go out on satellite TV." McColl was more concerned with the publicity coup for his team than Alex's personal glory. Nothing was going to spoil Peterboro McColl's great day, if he could help it. Certainly not a maverick who, to give him his due, had done everything that was asked of him, but somehow gave you the uneasy feeling he *could* fall off the tightrope.

McColl was a 100 per cent dedicated motor racing man who bitterly regretted that he had never been able to drive well enough to race his own cars and was obliged to hire others, whose commitment could never match his own. The world looked upon the drivers as heroes but what sort of heroes, however highly paid, hired themselves out to the highest bidder and changed their allegiance like film stars changed husbands?

The real heroes, the men who made the sport what it was, were epitomised by Enzo Ferrari. Even in their hour of triumph they had a lot to put up with.

"Just give me a break will you, Dick?" said Alex. "I've won the bloody world championship for you. I just need a few moments to myself to read a letter I've been waiting for for months. Is it really too much to ask? It may have a bearing on all sorts of things," he added, pointedly.

Unused to being defied by his drivers, McColl was furious. "And what am I supposed to tell people while you're holed up in here, reading that?"

"Tell 'em what you like. Tell 'em I'm on the bog. That I've got the runs - people do out here. Tell 'em I've fainted in the heat. I'm quite good at that. Remember Monaco?"

Scarcely able to contain his anger, McColl snapped: "Have you forgotten you're needed on the podium when they play the National Anthem?"

Alex stood up with a shamefaced grin. He had overstepped the mark this time and he knew it. Folding Caroline's letter neatly, he placed it carefully in the envelope, put it in a pocket, zipped up his overalls, and ruffled his dank hair into some sort of shape.

"OK, Dick. You win. But I must have a few moments to

read it after that."

"Right," said McColl, steering his driver out into the sun-drenched pit lane crowd with a proprietorial arm round his shoulder, "there's a time and place, you know."

* * *

There was often a febrile atmosphere in a grand prix pressroom when the chequered flag fell. No cars roared past and for the enthusiasts milling about all over the track waiting for the presentations, the show was over. The trial for the correspondents was about to begin. The photographers who had been sweating it out round the track with their heavy gear, came back to the pressroom for a rest and a gossip.

But the writing men now had to dig deep into their reserves of measured, accurate prose for the broadsheets and of hyperbole for the tabloids. Often against the clock. The sport's historians could pontificate at their leisure while the Fleet Street men, and their counterparts from other countries, had to produce in extremis. But how to collect one's thoughts with all this racket going on?

Mike Morgan had his tabloid paragraphs to write. His pages for the magazine could be done in the air conditioned comfort of the hotel later. He was determined to wring every drop of colour out of the great occasion. The crowning of an *English,* as opposed to a Scots, Australian or New Zealand world champion happened about once in a decade, if that. The fact that it was in such an exotic location, Jacarepagua, with its strange volcanic lumps dotting the green landscape, stirred his Welsh soul. Even if Alex Bastyan was an Englishman. He looked across to the presentations being made on the balcony on the opposite side of the track.

"Who's the gorgeous bird presenting the trophies?" he asked Randall who was watching through binoculars.

"How should I know? There's something on her sash but it doesn't look like a name. Never could speak Portuguese."

"Ask one of the Brazilians, you prat. He'll know. Use your sugar loaf, as they say in these parts."

Randall returned a few moments later. "Apparently, she's the Samba Queen of Brazil, no less, crowned at the carnival we've just missed. Her name's Wanda Moreno."

"Thanks, boyo," said Morgan, making a note of it. "But there's no call for 'apparently'. People either are or they aren't. 'Apparently' is woolly. Didn't they teach you anything on your NUJ training course?"

"I'll try to remember," said Randall huffily. He got really pissed off with Morgan at times, bollocking him like a provincial chief sub with a junior reporter. He thought he'd got away from all that, escaping from the claustrophobic world of local papers to a motor sport magazine.

"Only joking, boyo," said Morgan mildly. "It was good of you to get the name of the lovely." He re-focused the binoculars. "She *is* a little beauty."

"They're known for it in Brazil," said Randall.

"They are indeed. Her cups runneth over. Knowing Alex, I'm surprised he can resist raising such delectable goblets to his lips."

Morgan handed the binoculars back regretfully and tried to think of the intro for his tabloid report. Randall merely continued to enjoy the scene.

"'BRAZILIAN STUNNA CHATS UP CHAMP' should do it for you, Mike," he said.

"Very droll, boyo. That's only a picture caption. I want an intro, God dammit."

"Can't help you there. Look at this now, just goes to show there ain't no justice. Hector Bonfante – Brazil's own – has won the race. Juan Baltieri who's almost one of theirs from next door is second, yet it's Alex who really gets noticed."

"Obviously a girl who knows what she likes," said Morgan. "World champions, no less. Why bother with the monkeys when you've got the organ grinder?"

"No comment," said Randall. The Brazilian journalist he'd spoken to earlier came up with a grin and whispered in his ear.

After the man had gone back to his typewriter, Randall said: "It seems our Alex is in luck, getting all this attention. Miss Moreno is the local sex goddess. She's reputed to have bonked every bigshot and visiting VIP in Brazil. She's fussy though. Only goes for top celebs. You and I wouldn't stand a chance. Ah well, show's over and they're leaving the podium. That's funny... Hector and Juan are on their way over here for the press conference but Alex seems to be having a word with them as if to say he'll be along in a minute. Now he's disappearing into that timekeeper's office."

"What the hell's he up to?" demanded Morgan. "Here, let's have a shufti through those binocs again, boyo. Phew! There's cool for you. Didn't I say the man was a complete one-off? He's just won the world championship. The world's press – including you and me – is waiting to acclaim him on behalf of their readers and hear what he's got to say. What does he do? Keeps us all waiting while he reads something. You keep an eye on him. Could it be a letter? Let me know when he's finished it."

"He's folding it. Looks like it's all over now," said Randall a few minutes later. Morgan re-focused. "Now this is very interesting. Would you say Alex was a religious man?"

"Far from it. He doesn't behave like one."

"Precisely. There's hundreds of people milling around and all this racket going on yet he's standing stock still in that empty little room just above their heads. He's looking up and he's either in deep thought. Or can it be prayer? Good Evans! Now he's crossing himself! Whatever it was, the decision has been taken, he's leaving the room, coming down the stairs and on his way over. Most odd. That man is a complete contradiction and in 10 years I've never really understood him. Now, using your best powers of deduction, my dear Watson, who would you say sends a long letter with instructions for it to be hand-delivered at a certain time – to wit, the end of this sporting event – by an intermediary?"

"A woman Holmes?" replied Randall who enjoyed playing up to Morgan's imitations of Basil Rathbone as the Great Detective.

"I'll wager all Lombard Street to a china orange that it's *the* woman, Watson. His Irene Adler."

"Isn't it Caroline Tremayne in this case, Holmes?"

19

He read:

My darling Alex

I have not written before because the last thing in the world I want is to be a drag on you. I know how you hate wimpishness so I've kept quiet as a mouse since Monaco. But that doesn't mean I haven't been thinking of you every moment.

I've watched your wonderful success with oh! such mixed feelings. So glad for you, my darling, but so sad for Team Tremayne. Silly of me, I know, but I couldn't help wishing you were winning all those super races for us rather than McColl. But they can provide you with a winning car and we can't ...

Poor Freddie puts a brave face on things and we've been lucky with our new young driver, Pete Jankowski - French mother, Polish father, brought up in Clermont Ferrand and a Formula Two champion. I wonder what you think of what you've seen of him so far? That is, if you've had time to notice the back end of the grid, these days.

You know how you used to hate Teo-Nicolas so much? Well, he's one happy little Frenchman, forever getting into huddles with young Pete, telling him what to do. I reckon the Banger thinks that he's got one more season with us before he starts knocking on the Brabham, McLaren or Lotus motor home doors.

I suppose I've always known that Formula One is the most important thing in Freddie's life – as it is with all you men – and I come a poor second. I don't know which is worse for him, watching your success with McColl or his general misery over you and me. He's known about US for ages, apparently but said nothing until that dreadful day when you and he had The Showdown. That's the one aspect of all this that makes me feel not quite so badly about the way <u>we've</u> behaved.

Knowing Freddie, I'm sure it wasn't a conscious decision to turn a blind eye and 'sacrifice' me to keep you on side. Much more likely that he just sort of put it all to the back of his mind and somehow hoped it would all go away. To think otherwise is somehow to accuse him of acting like a man who's been pimping for his own wife.

I won't have anyone – especially you – thinking that of him. I know how brusque and decisive you can sometimes be and I do hope you didn't say anything to him you'd regret. Freddie didn't deserve what we did to him and we should be as kind to him as possible.

The trouble is we're both married to the wrong people and belong rightfully to each other, not me to Freddie and you to Olivia. I really thought I loved Freddie till you came along but I don't think you've ever really loved Olivia, from what you say.

I was so sorry to hear of her father's death. Stan Heyworth was a lovely man and will be much missed on the motor racing scene, so jolly and uncomplicated. You'd never think he'd built up and run such a huge business. I sent my condolences and didn't get a reply from Olivia, hardly surprising in the circs, I suppose, but Edna sent me a nice note.

The purpose of all this is to wish you all the luck in the world and to say how I've missed you since May 26. You notice

I haven't mentioned THE SLAP up to now. If it bothered you it hasn't bothered me. My pride was hurt more than anything and I blubbed like a silly schoolgirl with rage and frustration. More damage was done by running mascara than anything.

You were right. It was madness to have been making love when Freddie could've turned up at any moment and you had a grand prix in a few hours. The trouble was that I was aching for you physically like a real pain and wanted you to do it to me over and over again and I wouldn't've cared if His Holiness the Pope had walked in. You see what you've done to this once devout convent-educated girl?

I'm not religious any more. Wonderful, lustful sexuality implanted in my very psyche by you has driven out whatever mimminy-pimminy spirituality I once had as a hangover from a strict upbringing. It's all your fault, my darling.

My parents would've warned me against men like you. I remember my old father saying I should distrust men who danced or played snooker too well as those were undoubted signs of a mis-spent youth. I suppose he could've added 'or made love too well' but I don't care. I just know what I like. S-e-x with you!

Ma and Pa were never any good at the birds and the bees stuff. Their generation seemed to find the whole process so embarrassing that you wonder our lot ever got born. I suspect half of them did it with the lights off, never saw each other naked and always locked the bathroom door.

I'm sure you were right when you quoted some wise old bird as saying we should gather our sexual rosebuds in May because impotence and menopause await us in September, let alone eternity in December. The last thing I want to do is to put pressure on you but I'm not so young as I was and if I'm to give you those beautiful daughters we talked about, don't forget that the biological clock waits for no one.

I've forced myself to keep away from the circuits although I've promised myself a trip to Japan for the last race, come what may. I never used to go to every race as most of my work was done beforehand and I felt I needed a break but my self-imposed exile is hurting far more than I expected. I should've known how addictive the whole business becomes after a few years. Another reason for not being too hard on poor Freddie.

It's you I miss more than I can say. I'm not cut out for celibacy. Millions may be but I'm not. I know women are supposed to say how much they want comfort, companionship and to be cherished and all that stuff. Of course I need that but what I need most – and am deprived of – is marvellous moist-making, nipple-tingling sex with you.

When you touch me and give me so much pleasure, compared with poor Freddie's clumsy fumblings once in a blue moon even in the old days, I know what being loved really means. I used to be the happiest, most sexually fulfilled woman in the world. At intervals. Now I'm desolate.

I suppose that in spite of being liberated, emancipated and all the other 'ateds' of the 1980s, we women are still in hock to our hormones. I know I am. Me, the super-cool professional businesswoman helping to run a multi-million pound motor racing enterprise, now reduced to what the tabloids would call your 'sex slave'.

I can't remember who Pandora was and what was in the box she wasn't supposed to open but could it have been a metaphor for female sexuality? What makes us dangerous to you men is when we've been aroused from our torpor and become sexually rapacious. Or in my case these days, frustrated.

Poor Alex. You must think all this woman's talk is a terrible load of rot. I gather some women gossip to each other about their sex lives in the most shaming detail, particularly where male anatomical dimensions are concerned - no complaints in THAT department! But I don't have those sort of friends, always having been in a man's world. I can't talk about you to anyone but you. So please forgive me.

I'm in England fretting while you're in Brazil with the world championship at stake. I debated long and hard whether

*to write to you at all and eventually worked out a little
stratagem. I enclosed this in a letter to Dick McColl with a
fervent plea for him to give it to you the moment you stepped
out of the car at Jacarepagua, win or lose.*

*I wanted so much to be part of you at that moment. The
last thing I wanted was to be a distraction during your race
preparation and knew you wouldn't have time to think of me.
But afterwards I wanted to be in your thoughts. As you are
always in mine.*

*By the time you're reading this you may well be world
champion. You deserve it and I've been full of admiration for
the single-minded professionalism with which you've driven
for McColl. The best man in the best car has always been an
unbeatable combination in our business.*

*I have wished you the Brazilian GP and the world
championship with all my heart. There are two goals in our
game. Don't forget I used to play schoolgirl hockey at county
level. That's where I got the scar on my left knee that you like
to kiss better. The other goal is ME. I'm here, wide open, the
goalie is prostrate and there's only centre half Olivia to stop
you scoring. Isn't that what young guys say when they 'pull a
bird?' What an expression!*

*I'm not presenting you with an ultimatum. Women don't
do that to their men in Formula One. 'Stand By Your Man',
as the lady with several husbands sings.*

*Freddie and I are finished and I don't know which of us
feels the worst about it. In a funny sort of way we still love
each other and always will. Do you know what hurt most? He
told me an old feller like him ought to have known that he
couldn't have held on forever to anyone as 'beautiful as me'.
Especially when there were so many guys like you around in
Formula One. Was there an inference that if it wasn't you, it
could've been someone else or am I being hyper-sensitive?
One is at such times.*

*How do you think that made me feel? We both know we
can't go on living together when so much polluted water has*

flowed under the bridge of our marriage. What a Bridge of Sighs and I know I did all the polluting and betraying. Freddie was just dear old Freddie.

Which leaves you and Olivia. Only you and she know what's going on there. There's nothing I can say or do except to say over and over again that I love you - whatever she says, thinks or feels.

Now to the practicalities. The lawyers are working out the details. Freddie's kindly said I can keep the house at Bandol that we only used one week in the year and I'm going there tomorrow to smarten it up as I'm going to stay there for a while to sort myself out. Like you, I've always loved France and shall probably settle there and become a little old lady...

I shall wait for you as long as it takes but don't leave it too long if I'm to give you the beautiful daughters. You're 36 and I'm 34. I can't offer you the thrills of the race track and the cheers of the multitudes but I can offer you a life of peace and quiet and sex (periods and pregnancies excepted) with love continuing for ever.

Assuming you have clinched it in Rio, I can only ask after all this womanly waffle which has probably bored you to tears:

Is it to be me now or another season in Formula One?

With all my love always.

Caroline

20

Hector Bonfante and Juan Baltieri were still answering their routine and sometimes fatuous questions, good-naturedly aware that until Alex arrived they were just the warm-up act for the main attraction.

He took his seat at the table, reached across to shake hands, murmured his apologies and prepared to face world champion's ordeal by press conference. The interrogation began.

"When did you know the title was yours, Alex?"

"I didn't. I never count races until the chequered flag drops. I had a brake problem – what a time to get it – and it was just a question of hoping I could hold off Banger Thibault. I can be magnanimous now. No need to refer to him as the ex-team mate from hell. But there was no way I was going to catch these two guys."

"How does it feel to be world champion?"

"Tiring. It's been one helluva season."

"What are your future plans?"

"Immediately, to go back to the hotel in Rio, have a bath

and sink a bottle of champagne - and I don't mean the thimbleful from the mini-bar. After that I've got some phone calls to make."

"What about next season?"

"What about it?"

The Formula One press corps had got used to taciturn answers from Alex Bastyan but this caused a *frisson*.

"You'll be driving for McColl next year?"

"You said that, I didn't," Alex told the questioner from the French sports newspaper L'Equipe.

"Does that mean you won't be driving for McColl next season?"

"Yes."

The room erupted. Dick McColl, Chuck Giordano and Linda were stunned. They had pulled up chairs and joined the platform once their man was centre stage. The British journalists now weighed in. After all, he was their world champion.

"Yes, you will be or yes, you won't be, Alex?" This was a stentorian demand from Patrick Mennem, the man from the Daily Mirror, from the back of a room buzzing with chatter.

"Yes, I won't be, Pat."

"In that case," demanded The Guardian's Eric Dymock in his forthright Scottish way, "who are you driving for?"

"No one."

This was unprecedented. A world champion announcing his retirement at his post-race press conference. The hubbub in the room continued as Dick McColl and Chuck Giordano retired to a corner in urgent and agitated conversation. Suddenly confronted with a public relations nightmare, Linda joined them, her brain in fast rewind, trying to recall everything she'd ever been taught about damage limitation. How could the man do this? Then she was aware Alex was speaking.

"I guess I owe everyone an explanation. Not least my team and sponsors but they will confirm that my contract was from Hockenheim onwards to the end of this season only. I deliberately didn't commit myself beyond that because I wanted to see how things went. Don't forget, this was all new and wonderful for me, only having been with Team Tremayne for my entire Formula One career. Fortunately, things didn't go too badly ..."

This produced some smiles but most of the journalists were bemused. World champions didn't retire, just like that. Alex Bastyan had a reputation for eccentricity but this was absurd. Some of the British journalists who were not among his more fervent admirers had grown a little tired of trying to make allowances for him and explain his odd behaviour to their international colleagues. Pocket tape recorders were being held up all over the room to catch what he was saying for future reference and dissection while the camera shutters whirred and clicked at the platform party.

"I don't think many of us can understand this," said Eric Dymock. "You've won the world championship. McColl is the team to beat so why not carry on for another season and possibly do it again?"

"If only life were that simple, Eric. The most difficult decision any sportsman ever has to make is when to quit. There are few sadder spectacles in sport, I think, than the driver, boxer, athlete or whoever, who goes on too long and gets beaten by men he wouldn't've given houseroom to in his prime. Let's just say I don't want to fall into that trap. I've waited bloody ages for this success and I want to enjoy it untarnished by defeat in future years. The only way to ensure that is by quitting while you're ahead. Don't the comedians say, 'always leave 'em laughing'? I think a driver should always quit while the world thinks he's a winner."

If this didn't satisfy the journalists, particularly the Italians, the Peterboro McColl contingent was seething. When she was able to get a whispered word in edgeways, Linda pleaded for the softly-softly approach and no display of anger at what was obviously a gross and public betrayal by this unpredictable Englishman. Thankfully, her boss decided he would do the talking.

Giordano, McColl and Linda had resumed their places at the table. Hector Bonfante was taking a closer interest in the proceedings now he realised that his own chances next season were being enhanced. He readily pushed the microphone down the table at Giordano's request.

The swarthy little Italian-American stood up. "Gennelmen, as the chairman of the sponsors, I think we should give the noo world champion time to collect his thoughts. He's had one helluva tough race just now and a traumatic season. He stepped in under tragic circumstances and no one could've done better. Make no mistake about it, Alex did us proud and we're very grateful.

"It's true he was only contracted to us for half the season but we always regarded that as a formality. But it seems this guy is as smart at the law as he is in a race car. He must've read every line and struck out all references to future options on his services. I seem to remember being told something about this at the time but didn't pay all that much attention. All that mattered was getting him to Hockenheim in a few days in our car. But I'm still gonna fire our goddam useless lawyers for not getting him tied up tighter than a bull's ass in fly time."

This produced a laugh and lowered the tense atmosphere. Linda nodded appreciatively. This was good damage limitation PR. She shuddered to think what would be happening if the irascible Dick McColl had been let loose with the microphone.

"Getta loada this guy," continued Giordano with ungrudging admiration. "He didn't have an agent or lawyer with him but he outsmarted our legal guys and we pay them mega bucks. It just didn't occur to us he wasn't going to be with us next season – whatever the goddam contract said. But we had to let it go. There was no time for chewin' the fat over the legal niceties. The main thing was to get the car adjusted to fit him – fortunately there was no big hassle there – and get him briefed.

"Dick did a great job and we all know the result. He was

on pole at Hockenheim, won the race and has won most every race since. He's just the winningest guy! So no son-of-a-bitch bothered about the small print in his contract. I know you press boys like to speculate like junk bond salesmen about who's driving what next season. The ballyhoo usually starts by July, if not before. Hell, you know that better'n I do.

"Did any of you come up to me or Dick and ask us. 'Who's your number one for next year?' If you did, I sure as hell forget it. You were so busy watchin' a dream team that was winnin' race after race that you took it for granted. You guys are just as bad as we are. You just *assumed* he was signed up and there were certainly no challengers to the guy who was winning everything in sight. I guess we assumed it too. That's a dangerous business. Assumptions are for assholes. You might think it kinda strange that here we are, one race from the end of the season and we haven't got our number one driver signed for next year. What a way to run a race team, eh guys?"

Chuck Giordano produced a large handkerchief from the pocket of his green and white Peterboro McColl blouson and wiped the sweat off his chubby face. With his easy American approachability he was popular with colleagues and journalists alike and wielded the immense power of the Peterboro Chemical Corporation's wealth with a light hand.

Many wondered how two or three grand prix teams would survive if his dollars went elsewhere but they were safe so long as Charles Giordano had anything to do with it. He was a motor racing nut from way back who had a stableful of Ferraris at the ranch he was rarely able to visit in California.

"I think we can be forgiven after such a season," he went on, "and perhaps I won't be firin' those legal schmucks after all. I'm the guy in charge and the buck stops with me. Our aim was to carry on in the way Johnny Abati had begun the season for us. We achieved that, thanks to this wunnerful guy Alex here, and if he feels he's so tuckered out he needs to quit, well I guess that's up to him - if you're sure you mean it, Alex?"

"What can I say after all that, Chuck? You make me feel like the ultimate in ungrateful bastards." Alex could sense the mood of the press conference swinging away from him. Giordano was one of the best liked men in Formula One and he, Alex, was seen to be letting him down.

"But I'm afraid I've been thinking about retirement for two or three seasons. But thank you for the kind remarks. They're more than I deserve. I was called in to try to carry on Johnny Abati's work and win the title. That and no more. Thanks to a first-class car and excellent team work – *and* the luck that every world champion needs, I was able to deliver.

"But it hasn't been easy. Not that it ever is in this sport. There're all sorts of factors to consider here. There's my age – pushing 37 – triple world champions have retired younger than that. Then there's my lifestyle. The Playboy Driver some of you call me. There comes a point in every man's life when enough is enough. And I've reached it."

All over the room journalists were taking notes, most without shorthand scribbling furiously, others relying on tape recorders. This was a big story that would lead the world's sports pages. Although glad to have the unexpected angle of Alex's retirement, the British press corps cursed the three-hour time difference between Rio and London which would make them miss the first editions.

If only Alex had given them some inkling of all this they could have warned the sports desk and got more space allocated for their stories. Normally the sort of driver who made a Trappist monk seem garrulous, the bloody man was now giving them more good quotes than they could cope with.

"I've been lucky," he went on, "and I don't kid myself it's been anything but luck. If Johnny hadn't had that accident he'd be sitting here. But fate decreed otherwise and it's me. I've had my share of luck and there's no point in pushing it too far. Besides, there are too many examples of singleton champions who didn't exactly cover themselves in glory in later years. I want to go out on a high. At a moment like this. I also like the idea of retiring undefeated and not having to scrap too hard with young guys like Hector and Juan any more. They're a decade younger than me and make me feel my age. I guess I'm getting old."

"But Aleex," implored an Italian journalist, "what are you going to do?"

"What am I going to do?" Alex paused and smiled wickedly. "Let's just say I'm retiring early to spend time with other men's families."

"That's it!" whispered Mike Morgan to Pete Randall, sitting next to him in the second row. "He *is* going to get it together with Caroline Tremayne. That's all I need for my tabloid."

The British journalists just fell about laughing while their international colleagues looked nonplussed. Dick McColl, who had been last in line when the senses of humour were handed out, found such levity intolerable. His balled right fist smashed into left palm with enough noise under the table to make those sitting nearby look at him sharply.

He was beside himself with rage but he also knew a lot of cameras were ranged on him, recording his reaction to Alex Bastyan's shock announcement. Controlling his fury at such a public snub was impossible. How any driver could walk way from the best seat in Formula One was beyond McColl. It was humiliation he could neither forgive nor forget.

Alex waited for silence in a room that was loath to settle down. This was the strangest post-race press conference that even the most senior International Racing Press Association member could remember.

"Perhaps I'd better explain," said Alex. "In England the slightest whiff of scandal or of a sexual peccadillo means that a politician has to resign. In France you wouldn't vote for a man who didn't have a mistress? *C'est vrai n'est-ce pas?*"

The French journalists grinned and nodded.

"In hypocritical Britain it's different and the politician

caught in the wrong bed, apologises publicly, his wife stands by him and he retires to spend more time with his family. Thanks to you tabloid boys - well your gossip column colleagues - being so assiduous, I enjoy a reputation that could get any French politician elected President. I just adapted the saying to suit my circumstances."

"I've never seen him like this," said Randall. "He's like a man with a great weight off his mind. I bet we're the only ones who've twigged it about Caro–"

"Shh," said Morgan, placing a finger to his lips.

"Now if you'll excuse me," said Alex, getting up to go.

Linda went over to him quickly and whispered in his ear. Alex nodded.

"Sorry, I'm not used to this sort of thing." To the room at large, he said: "Any more questions?"

"Won't you be having *any* connection with motor sport?"

"I doubt it, Pat," said Alex. "Let me explain why. When you've had the immense good fortune to enjoy almost any activity at the top level, nothing else will do. An old mate of mine flew fast jets for the RAF and even did a tour with the Red Arrows. He loved the Air Force and thought he would be there till he was 45. But he was axed under some cost-cutting scheme and now sells Rolls-Royces. I asked him if he missed flying and he said he missed it like hell. When I said why not join a flying club and fly at weekends, he said that when you've flown the best, with the best, everything else is peanuts. I know how he felt.

"How do you follow Formula One? With all its faults, there's nothing like it. There's nothing like the buzz of winning a Formula One race, simply because it's so bloody difficult. Getting there is difficult, taking part is difficult, winning is difficult. To be world champion is the ultimate. Don't forget I started much later than most and came up the hard way, whatever some people say.

"The only thing I seem to have missed is Karts but I did my time in Formula Ford, Formula Three, Formula 3000 and tin-tops and sports cars by way of light relief. To put it crudely, I'm knackered. I've survived but I've had enough."

The room was quieter now but sensing the need to throw the more disapproving dogs some sort of a bone, he added: "The only thing that might tempt me back is Le Mans – it would be great to do well there."

He pressed on, now that it seemed the pack wasn't baying quite so fiercely for his blood. "Somebody asked me earlier what I was going to do. I can tell you what I'm not going to do. I'm not the kind of guy who could run a racing school. I don't suffer fools gladly and I'm far too bad tempered and irritable. I'm not going to try to run an airline – I can't fly. I'm not even going to be an international entrepreneur and businessman because I don't know anything about making money."

This was met with good natured mock groans of sympathy for the poor millionaire, which he acknowledged with a grin. The Italian journalists, particularly, felt short-changed by the driver they had dubbed *IL PANTERO NEGRO,* the Black Panther. Some of them had even berated Ferrari in the past for not trying to sign up the man many regarded as the best of the current drivers never to have won the championship. Now he had won it, he was walking away. Where was his *corragio?* Signor Ferrari would never approve of a man who did that. It was probably just as well Bastyan had never signed for The Scuderia after all.

Alex got the distinct impression that they thought he had lost his bottle. If they wanted to think that, so be it. Italians were jolly people so long as everything went their way. If it didn't and you wanted to do something else, they tended to lose interest. His popularity in Italy would fall like a dodgy share but what did it matter now?

"So we won't be seeing Alex Bastyan at any grand prix in the future?" said David Benson in his gravelly voice. It was half statement, half question.

"That depends."

"On what, Alex?" The millions of Daily Express motor sport enthusiasts weren't going to be fobbed off that easily if the lanky Beaverbrook bloodhound had anything to do with it.

"On whether I can get the odd pit pass out of Bernie," replied Alex with an engaging grin. This produced another titter. "Seriously though, David, I hope to be around from time to time but strictly as a casual observer. That doesn't mean I'm going to be writing a newspaper column. I can't write - at least not like you blokes, thank God. And if there're no more questions I really must get back into Rio and give you scribes time to write your articles. Don't forget it's Bastyan with a Y."

"Why indeed?" said Randall.

Alex stood up, shook hands with a still shell-shocked Chuck Giordano, kissed the startled Linda on one cheek, avoided Dick McColl who was now talking pointedly to Hector Bonfante, gave a half wave to the room at large and walked quickly to the door. He brushed aside those who followed him, tape recorders at the ready, with a firm:"That's all gentlemen. I've said all I'm going to say.".

"We know why he's going, don't we?" Morgan murmured. "But I wonder how many of our hotshot colleagues do? I reckon I've got an angle for my report in the old Muckraker that'll get a few news desk rockets winging their way to some of our old mates tomorrow. The trouble is, how to word it? These tabloid sub-editors have never heard of grey or maybe. Everything's black and white and definite. Your inference is their inscription set in tablets of stone. Excuse me while I get on with it, boyo. We haven't got time on our side."

"I'll leave you in peace," said Randall. "Thank God I don't have to file for a tabloid. But did you see the look on McColl's face just now? That's another implacable enemy Alex's made. Still, what does it matter now he's going. And what about poor old Freddie Tremayne – if we have to feel sorry for Formula One team owners. He does seem to have missed all the ladders and overdosed on the snakes, not only lost his wife but had his racing season screwed up as well."

"Alas, poor Freddie," said Morgan. "I can just imagine the headline they'll put on my piece in tomorrow's paper: ACE QUITS RACES FOR WIFE OF EX-BOSS."

"He won't see it," Randall replied. "They don't seem to get many tabloids out here. I've only seen The Telegraph and The Times, and they've been a few days old."

"But other papers'll probably follow it and poor old Freddie'll be given hell by the London boys when he steps off the plane at Heathrow. Can't you just imagine it? 'Give us a statement Mr Tremayne. Anything to say about the new world champion running off with your wife?' 'When did you first know Alex Bastyan and your wife were an item?' 'Are you going to divorce her?' Poor old sod, he doesn't deserve all that. Alex'll get it too."

"I don't know about Freddie," said Randall, "but Alex can take care of himself. He's a great guy and we all love him dearly but you've got to admit the bugger deserves everything he gets."

"Don't we all?"

"I'm sure you're right," said Randall, "about Alex deciding to jack it all in after getting Caroline's letter. But there's something that puzzles me; he's the least religious man in the world, so why on earth should he cross himself after reading it?"

"Because, boyo, racing drivers are as superstitious as medieval peasants. You'll find bullfighters, mountaineers, bike racers, all those taking part in potentially life-threatening activities usually are. One man will only get into his car from the left side, another has to wear his lucky balaclava, no matter how old it is, or his special gloves. Another will never race without his St Christopher round his neck. Because no driver would sit in a car with the number 13, there is no number 13. And don't forget Stirling always wanting number 7 on his cars.

"You get my drift? I'm not aware that Alex had any special

superstitions like that. It's not the sort of thing you can discuss anyway. But don't forget he had just decided to tell the world that he had completed his last grand prix."

"But there's still one to come," said Randall. "Japan in two weeks' time."

"Precisely! He was warding off the evil eye in case Brazil really was his last."

21

After the umpteenth time, Alex finally got through from the Caesar Park Hotel to the Tremayne house near Lambourn in Berkshire. A female foreign voice answered sulkily in parrot fashion: "Tremayne residence. Meester Tremayne ees in Brazil, Meesis Tremayne ees in France." This must be the little Filipino perisher who's been on the phone to Manila or wherever for the past three hours while I've been trying to get through, he thought.

"Thank you. I know about Mr Tremayne. I'm calling from Rio myself. But I urgently need to speak to Mrs Tremayne in France. Can you give me her telephone number, please. It's very important."

"I not know eet," said the voice.

"But it must be written down somewhere. On a memory board or something?"

"I not know," the girl repeated infuriatingly.

"But you must know if you work for Mrs Tremayne. She goes there sometimes and she must leave the number where she is in case you need to speak to her."

"I no work here," the girl said. "My friend Maria, she work here. I am like baby sitter for 'er."

Just my horrible luck, he thought. To get the help's helper. "Have you got a pencil there? Can you write this down?"

There was a noise at the other end which he took for assent.

"If Mrs Tremayne rings home please ask her to call Alex in Rio on 010 55 21 287 3122. That's the Caesar Park Hotel. Have you got that? Can you read it back to me? The name Alex and the number is what matters."

Surprisingly, the girl did. He felt much better disposed towards her. "Thanks very much. Sorry to have disturbed you. Good night."

Just as he put the phone down there was a knock on the door.

"Who is it?" he demanded. If it was a delegation headed by McColl and company he would refuse to open it. He felt that shagged out and brassed off.

"It is your Queen," said a soft female voice.

Queen? What queen? Sod this Victoria and Albert lark, he thought. Nevertheless intrigued, he put on a bathrobe, went to the door and opened it to find himself staring down the magnificent cleavage of a small dark beauty who looked vaguely familiar.

"You no remember me?" she said looking up with an entrancing smile. "I am the samba queen who gave you your prize at Jacarepagua. My name is Wanda Moreno. You not know me because I wear different clothes and not the high shoes. They so uncomfortable. May I come in?"

As he stood aside, she brushed past him giving him the full benefit of her sensuous perfume and a view of the tops of her wonderful breasts. She was simply dressed in an off-the-shoulder white peasant style blouse, a short black skirt and a wide red belt that clinched her handspan waist.

"This is an unexpected pleasure," was all he could think of to say. The need for sleep and irritation at not being able to get hold of Caroline on the phone were uppermost in his mind.

If he hadn't been so tired he would have appreciated the irony of being brassed-off at having such a beautiful woman calling at his hotel room late at night.

"Won't you sit down? Would you like a drink?" he asked, peering into the mini-bar. She accepted a Campari and then walked about with a proprietorial air.

Alex fell back into the room's most comfortable chair wondering what this strange little beauty was going to do next. He didn't have long to wait.

She went over to the bedside and picked up the silver framed head-and-shoulders photograph of Caroline that travelled everywhere with him. She then took it over to the standard lamp where there was more light. "Your wife?" she asked.

"No." He added pointedly: "It's the woman I love."

"She very lovely. Not like pale English lady. She could be from Brazil!"

"Our women aren't all English roses, fair haired, blue eyed and freckled who turn bright red in the sun," he said defensively.

Caroline and he had often joked about her exotic un-English appearance and glorious skin with its all-over permanent light tan. She liked to think it was due to the days of the Raj and a female ancestor having a romantic liaison with some lusty Indian princeling. Her forbears had followed the flag and made the family fortunes building cotton mills out east.

Wanda Moreno then sat on the edge of the bed and fiddled with the radio/TV controls let into the bedhead. When she had found a station pumping out the sort of Latin-American dance music she liked, she adjusted the volume to a subtle background sound and came over to him.

"You like to dance?"

"Not now, thanks. Besides, I'm not much good."

"I show you how. I am samba queen," she said proudly.

"I'm sorry. I'm just too tired. It's been one helluva day."

Realising he was adamant, she pouted, shrugged and then sat down at his feet, resting her head and arms on his knees. She then looked up at him as soulfully as a labrador waiting for its walk.

This is ridiculous, he thought. She thinks she's here for the night. It was time to tell this lovely little piece a few home truths and kick her out.

"I'm sorry to be such a party pooper," he said. "I can assure you it's not my normal style but you've caught me at a bad moment after the most momentous day of my life. It's been a traumatic weekend. I've won the world championship and now I'm going to retire and settle down with the woman I love."

"Retire? But you not an old man. My pappa he retire but he 60. How can you geeve up your life with such –"

"Glamour, travel and excitement?"

She nodded.

"I've had enough excitement to last me a lifetime. You do in motor racing. As to the glamour, it has its moments, being in places like Rio but there's nothing very glamorous about endless test laps at Silverstone on a wet autumn day – and I've got some of that next week. Then we've got to go to Japan, where it's nearly always raining at this time of year, for the last race. As to the joys of travel, all I see is airports, hotels and circuits. After a few years they all look alike. There's never time to see anything of the country you're in. Rio's different, of course. It's great, but all I've seen is the road from the airport to the hotel here and from here to the circuit. I haven't seen the view from Sugar Loaf mountain or from Corcovado."

Alex yawned extravagantly. "Half the time you don't know what country it is. As to most of the hotels you might as well be in the Gatwick Hilton for all the local atmosphere you get ... they're all the same with the bog seats sanitised for your convenience and the showercaps and the chocolate on the pillow. Who the hell wants chocolate when you've just cleaned your teeth to go to bed? And the silly rollers in the corridors to clean your shoes ... Monte Carlo's about the only place that seems to have any decent hotels left and the Villa d'Este, of course on Como ... or is it Lake Garda I can never remember but it's all marvellous ...."

His eyes closed and he nodded off. Then he was aware she was standing over him, trying to pull him to his feet.

"I think it is time we go to bed," she said.

"Not so much of the *we*," he said, taking her gently by the arm and steering her towards the door.

Wanda jerked her head towards the bedside table with the picture of Caroline.

"She not know what we do in this room," she said petulantly.

"Maybe not, but I will," he said, without feeling the least bit priggish.

"I'm sorry, my dear, but I really must get some sleep. And so should you. Good night and thanks for looking in." He kissed her on both cheeks, let her out into the corridor and shut the door with a sigh of relief.

Too tired even to remember about the security chain, he flung off the bathrobe, fell backwards stark naked on to the bed and was instantly asleep.

22

He was dreaming. He had a splendid erection and a woman's soft fingers were strumming on the shaft, slow then fast, pausing when it seemed he could bear the pleasurable torment no longer. The next moment everything changed and he was thrusting into the moist, pliant body of a beautiful olive skinned woman. But he couldn't see her face. Was it the same lovely who had been masturbating him so skilfully? Who was she? It was now the most glorious fuck he'd had for a long time, but worryingly, it wasn't with Caroline. The exquisite pleasure was diminished by a sense of loss and guilt that it wasn't Caroline. Why wasn't it Caroline giving him so much pleasure? This was cruel when he missed her so much. Who was this?

With his cock enveloped in peerless sensations he was in that half-waking, half-sleeping mode, aware that this was the wet dream to end all wet dreams. It had to be nature's revenge for the months of abstinence.

Torn between the dream state and wakefulness he opened his eyes. Sunlight was streaming into the room and lying on his back he couldn't believe what he saw. Straddling him, thighs splayed, leaning back and toying with the erect nipples on breasts out of scale with the rest of her slender little body, was – Wanda Moreno.

He reached up and felt her satin skin. She was real. It was no longer a dream. But how?

"Shh," she whispered, laying a carmine tipped finger on his lips. "I tell you later. Now is for loving – not speaking."

She resumed the motion of his dream, rising and falling rhythmically. Almost the full length of his shaft was exposed before she sank lubriciously down until their pubic hair meshed.

All the while her muscles squeezed and released him tantalisingly. Soon the rhythm changed and she began lunging wildly, rotating her hips in a mindless effort to extract the ultimate pleasure from him. Then with a gasp she flung herself forward lying full length on him, pumping, pumping with her hips.

"Hold the breasts, bite the nipples," she commanded in a husky voice that was barely recognisable as a woman's. Finally she collapsed with a groan that turned into a cry as his seed pulsated into her with exquisite spasms.

* * *

It had been very passionate sex – on Wanda's part. But Caroline had taught him that sex without a loving commitment was merely animal. Alex felt guilty not only for having enjoyed it but for having done it at all. But he hadn't. Even a saint wouldn't've been able to withdraw at the stage things were when he woke up. It was more than flesh and blood could stand. He'd been assaulted by this mad Moreno woman! But how? He distinctly remembered sending her home the night before.

"How did I get in?" she said at last when her breathing

had returned to normal. "You were so tired last night, you never see when you put me out – like I was the cat, or sumsing. The key was on the table by the door and I pick it up. I wait outside for only a minute, open the door and see you sleeping like baby. I come in and lie down beside you and sleep also. In the morning I go to the bathroom and when I come back and lie awake beside you I see you become ready for love. It make me feel vairy sexy. I could not resist. I play with you and still you sleep. Then I make myself ready, rubbing with my fingers. I put you inside me so gentle. I wonder how long it would be before you come? I think I maybe come before you wake up ..."

"It was all giving me an incredible dream, I can tell you that."

"But you men, when you are leetle boys you 'ave these dreams no, and you come in your sleep? This was real, *querida*."

Too bloody real by half, he thought. How on earth was anyone going to believe it? Most important, how was he going to tell Caroline? How would anyone believe that he'd put the woman out of his room, that she'd got back in during the night and that he'd woken up to find *her* screwing *him!*

Who the hell did the bloody woman think she was - even if she was the samba queen of Brazil - barging into a chap's hotel room and helping herself to his morning glory? Was nothing sacred? The whole thing was so ludicrous he found himself stifling a giggle. How old Mike Morgan would laugh if he ever got to hear of it and what tabloid headlines it would make. RACE ACE RAPED BY SAMBA QUEEN was certainly a new slant. Perhaps this was the new Latin-American feminism. Men as sex objects and playthings of female passion? What a turn-up. He might've enjoyed it more if he wasn't a reformed character.

Reaching across the recumbent Wanda for a drink of water from the bedside table he caught sight of Caroline's picture and turned it to the wall.

"Why do you do that?" Wanda demanded sulkily.

"Why do you think," he said. "Though it's a bit bloody late now."

"You feel shame, making love with me?" she asked.

"Of course not. Well yes, I suppose I do. Oh hell, you'd never understand."

He got up, went into the bathroom for a pee and a thorough wash. Unprotected sex with women he didn't know well had never been part of his repertoire. Even if he'd had a condom he couldn't have used it with this sex-crazed piece.

"I'm sorrry, er – Wanda," he called over his shoulder. "I didn't mean to hurt your feelings just now but you don't understand how much I love Caroline. I haven't been unfaithful to her. Two things and two things only have mattered to me this season: winning the world championship, which you know all about since yesterday, and being faithful to Caroline about which you can know bugger all," he added sotto voce.

"I've been celibate – that means I haven't fucked anybody – since May 26, the date of the Monaco Grand Prix. All my efforts have been put into trying to win the title since I inherited Johnny Abati's seat in the McColl. He was the guy everyone thought was going to be world champion this year. He didn't make it. He got killed at Dijon.

"With luck and a little bit of help from my friends I've done it. And now I'm going to settle down and spend the rest of my life with the woman I love. You've no idea of the aggro, the trouble, I'm going through because I want to do that, Wanda. Half the world lives with the woman it loves, why can't I? Now I've got someone to live for who cares about me, I've suddenly discovered I don't want to go on risking my neck any more. Why the hell should I?"

Wrapping the bathrobe round him he walked into the bedroom. "Sorry to rush you, but I can send for some breakfast and then I've got to dash and catch a plane."

There was no reply. The room was empty. Caroline's picture no longer faced the wall but stark on the white sheets was a tiny pair of black, lace-trimmed knickers.

"Silly bitch," he said with a grin, tossing them in the wastepaper basket.

23

Alex could only cat-nap on the flight back to London. The aura of hostility from Dick McColl in the next seat was palpable and most of the other team members seemed to be avoiding his eye. Despite having won the drivers' world championship – the combination of his and Abati's victories had also secured the constructors' title for McColl – Alex knew he was not flavour of the month. As far as the team was concerned his glory time had lasted the 45 minutes from the time he got out of the car to his announcement at the press conference at Jacarepagua.

Only Peter Foot had come up to him and shaken him warmly by the hand. "I don't blame you, Alex," he'd said. "You've done us proud and Johnny couldn't've done better. If you want to quit now while you're ahead, good luck to you. I remember how glad James was to pack it in and Jochen would've retired at the end of the '70 season, if he'd lived. Frankly, I don't know what all the fuss is about – although you can't say that round here."

"Injured pride, I reckon," Alex had replied. "I don't think

anyone's ever given Dick McColl the brush-off before and he can't take it. Like a lot of people, our Dick can dish it out but he can't take it."

Between the fitful bouts of sleep, he planned his course of action over the next few days before he had to be at Silverstone for pre-Japanese Grand Prix testing.

It was cold and grey and miserable when the Varig Airlines Boeing 747 touched down at Heathrow. "Welcome to sunny Britain," joked Peter Foot as they walked the endless corridors to baggage reclaim.

"If there are any reporters out there, Pete, can you tell 'em I missed the plane or something?"

"Don't be daft, Alex, they know what you look like. Let me think now if you want to dodge the blighters ... You're just in jeans, a shirt and a sweater and they'll expect us to stick together. Your best bet, I reckon, is to let the rest of us wearing all this Peterboro McColl team gear go on ahead."

He looked around at the other passengers in the passport queue. "Why don't you try and secrete yourself in with that group of schoolgirls as if you're one of their teachers? If there is a load of press out there they'll expect you to be with Dick McColl and me and the rest of the team. You might just get away with it."

"Good thinking, Pete. It's worth a try. I'll have to be Captain von Trapp or whatever his name was."

The ploy worked. Fortunately, the woman checking passports was neither a motor racing enthusiast nor an avid newspaper reader and the new world champion returned home unrecognised. Head down amid the giggling schoolgirls he caught a glimpse of Peter Foot arguing the toss with a crowd of camera-toting, notebook waving angry journalists as he edged past.

Easing his luggage trolley through the card-carrying chauffeurs desperately seeking So-and So, Alex made his way straight to the Air France ticket desk in Terminal Two to get on a plane for Marseilles the next day. Fortunately it wasn't fully booked. He then took the courtesy bus to the off-airport Excelsior Hotel for an overnight stay. There was no point in going all the way back to Warminster. Once in the hotel room he threw himself on the mercy of Pat Russell, the receptionist at Tremayne's and begged her to give him the number of the house near Bandol.

"I don't think I ought to give it to you, Alex. You're bad news round here," she said. "Even if you are world champion. Heartiest congratulations by the way."

"Thanks," he said. "I know. I'm bad news at McColl, too. I've just quit on them. I'm packing it all in for good. Caroline and I are getting it together. She's written to me to say she's gone to Bandol but she didn't give me an address or phone number.

"I'm booked on the plane tomorrow but I don't know how to find her when I get there. You've gotta help me. Please Pat!"

"Oh, all right. But I'd get into terrible trouble if Freddie found out."

"I'm afraid it's all over as far as Freddie and Caroline are concerned and so is my marriage. I'm not proud of it, Pat, but that's the way things are. Caroline and I just both got it wrong the first time, I guess."

"Hold on a minute, Alex. I think I've got a number here somewhere: 010 33 35 42 86 78. I'm sure that's it. There's no address with it I'm afraid."

"That'll have to do. Bless you, Pat. You'll get your reward in heaven for helping to make the course of true love run smooth."

"I only hope it all works out for both of you. I just feel so sorry for Freddie - he's such a sweet old guy."

"Do you think we don't? But what can you do? Olivia's given me the heave. But nobody wants to be beastly to Freddie. It's just one of those things.

* * *

Caroline was waiting for him when he had cleared customs and passport control at Marseille-Provence airport. There was no mistaking her in a Liberty print dress, floppy straw hat and dark glasses, half a head taller than a group of black-garbed Arab women nearby.

She stood stock still as he walked towards her, only removing the glasses and smiling almost shyly. He noticed the signs of strain round her eyes and mouth. She's been going through it as well, he thought, before they fell into each other's arms without a word. They devoured each other with famished mouths and tongues, uncaring, heedless of the stares of passers-by, some envious, others censorious. Finally, they broke apart.

"Oh darling," she said. "You don't know how I've waited for this moment."

"Me too," he said and they both laughed. "Funny how you can never think of the right thing to say at the really important moments of your life. All I can say is how much I love you and how I thought this moment would never come. Even after I got you on the phone yesterday I didn't somehow believe it. That letter of yours was the turning point of my life. From next month after the Japanese Grand Prix I'm all yours."

"Don't make me cry," she said. "Not when we've just met again."

"What is there to cry about for heaven's sake?"

"All this sacrifice." She sniffed and replaced the dark glasses.

"You've just become world champion. But you're giving it all up – for me."

"I've done it for both of us," said Alex gruffly. "Well, for me really. I could only say it to you but you know why I gave up, Caroline? It was – don't laugh – to save my ruddy soul. Don't get me wrong. There've been wonderful guys who made it to the top in Formula One like Fangio and Jimmy. Johnny Abati was another but I could never be in their class as a driver or as a man. Not in a million years.

"They had God-given talent. I don't suppose it was ever a

struggle for them. I bet they never had to work at it like I did. I was no analytical test driver, as useful on the test track as I was in the race. Fangio could take a car apart and put it back together as well as any of his mechanics and Jimmy had his incredible rapport with Colin. And they were *natural* drivers. They drove as naturally as blackbirds sing.

"Nobody could ever say that about me. I drove the way a corncrake croaks. But I worked at it and tried to make it look easy and gradually people began to say I was good, but it never came naturally to me like it does to the greats. All that struggle, effort and single-mindedness made me a cantankerous old sod, someone who bonked his brains out by way of light relief. I sometimes wonder how many of those girls I was screwing ever twigged they were really walking talking psychiatrists' couches as far as I was concerned. Saving my sanity through sex ...

"Don't forget I started far later than most drivers who got to the top. I always thought of myself as the ultimate Avis swan. You know, the one trying hardest. Bogus serenity on the surface but paddling like a demented duck underneath. Making all that effort appear effortless took it out of me. And when the success wouldn't come with old Freddie's team it made me imposs-"

Caroline had never heard him talk like this before and went to interrupt.

"Don't deny it, old luv. I know it's true and so do you. Your letter was all I needed to tip me over the edge into making the right decision. OK so I'm world champion at last and I go on another year with a crown to defend? I'd be even more impossible, getting paranoid every time I didn't win, imagining plots and skulduggery in my own team, let alone sharp practice by the opposition. No. Being a retired champion is my only hope of trying to become a halfway decent human being. Other drivers can cope with the pressures and stay human. I can't. Know thyself, as they say."

Caroline placed a slender finger on his lips.

190

"No more, darling. Don't I have any say in all this? I know you and I love you."

"Thank God for that," he said, pulling her to him. "Life as a human being begins in my 37th year," he murmured into the lustrous shoulder-length raven hair. Then he stood back and searched her face anxiously. She tried to smile and looked near to tears again.

"What *am* I doing to you?" he said. "Airports aren't places to bare the soul and wring the withers. C'mon. We can't stand around here. First of all we scandalise the natives by necking in public and then you start blubbing. Frightfully un-British, old bean. And I don't like the way that gendarme with the sub-machine gun has been eyeing us. We'll either get shot or be asked to move on. Where's your car parked? I'm looking forward to seeing the French property."

Alex picked up his bag as Caroline led the way to the car park, saying: "Surely you remember those ghastly barbecues I tried to give when the French GP was at Le Castellet? The trouble was it was too far from the circuit or people couldn't find it. A lot of grub got wasted, I recall."

"If I'd been to a barbecue at the Tremayne holiday home in the South of France I'd've remembered it. It must have been in my wildman period when a bonk seemed a better bet than a barbie."

"Never mind, darling," she said. "I'm here now and you can bonk me ad infinitum. In between doing up the cottage, of course. It needs some tender loving care which I've now got time to give it. You'll be able to help."

"We've got all the time in the world for both," he said. "I give you fair warning. DIY is not my forte, but I promise to be an ace foreman keeping the local *ouvriers* up to the mark – or the franc more likely."

Caroline drove the little Peugeot hire car, windows open in the sunshine, along the twisting coast road through the little towns of Cassis, La Ciotat, and Les Lecques. Alex told her all about his battle for the championship and ended up confessing the episode of the samba queen.

"I believe you, though millions wouldn't," she said laughingly when he'd finished.

"You're just saying that to be nice to me," he said. "You don't really believe it for a minute. Who would? Let alone another woman. I find it hard to credit it myself but the little bitch really did snitch the key on the way out of the room and let herself in later when I was out cold."

"But you conveniently omitted to put the security chain on the door. That's the weakness of this whole story. Not that I'm disbelieving you, my sweet."

"I was shattered and I just forgot. For Pete's sake, I'd had a long and difficult race in intense heat with the title at stake. Then there was the fateful press conference where I took a lot of stick. You know how I hate all that public speaking crap. To cap it all I spent hours back at the hotel trying to get a number for you out here. I was knackered, not to put too fine a point on it. Even the hot bath and the bottle of champagne I sank with dinner via room service didn't pep me up. It just shows how far gone I was and how it's time I gave it all up. I was practically out on my feet when this sex bomb fronts up.

"I try to be reasonably polite and offer her a drink and a few minutes' chat before showing her the door. But what happens? She comes a big number about teaching me to samba, or something, and when I fall asleep on her in the chair, she suggests it's bedtime for both of us. I finally get rid of her with a chaste kiss on the cheek. Bugger me, the next thing I know she's on the job, humping me as if the end of the world is nigh."

"Poor woman!" said Caroline. "She was only behaving like most men. It must've been quite a shock when you turned her down. She must've got a very poor impression of English*men*. It probably confirmed the view – widely held in foreign parts – that you're a bunch of poofs who don't like women. Present company excepted, of course."

"I should bloody hope so."

"No. It's such an improbable tale, it has to be true, my love. Nobody could make that up. Certainly no man I've ever met could've pulled it out in those circumstances and I forgive you. What's more I respect and love you for telling me at all – most men wouldn't've done that."

She patted his knee affectionately and leaned across to kiss him on the cheek.

"Watch it!" he shouted as the little car swerved perilously close to an approaching van. "I've just discovered I want to live forever. I thought you did too."

* * *

That night they made love for the first time in months. Caroline was bitterly upset when he insisted on using a condom. "Why? You know how I hate those horrible rubber things." But she relented after he explained: "Just a temporary precaution post-Rio."

24

The few days with Caroline at Bandol were the happiest he could remember. There was life after Formula One. He had been so busy for the last decade, racing, testing, travelling, there had been no opportunity to share time with another human being, let alone the woman he loved.

He was pushing 40 and had been lucky, so far, to escape serious injury in one of the world's most dangerous sports. Now there was one more race in Japan and he would never sit in a grand prix car again.

What would he do with the rest of his life? He had promised Caroline he wouldn't race in Formula One any more but he was on record as saying he would like to do Le Mans. The next few weeks and months would be a learning curve as he found out how much he was going to miss the sport that had been everything to him for so long.

Renovating Caroline's lovely old cottage with its two foot thick stone walls, inadequate plumbing and heating was not a life's work. Nor was getting the grounds into shape although he was looking forward to the installation of a tennis court and a pool.

Jim Clark, he remembered, had always said racing drivers shouldn't be married. But plenty were. As he'd been, after a fashion. Some combined racing not only with marriage but even with parenthood. Though how they'd managed to concentrate when there were so many other considerations baffled him. Perhaps having families and other things to worry about, apart from the endless frustrations and disappointments in the cockpit, kept them on a more even keel than he'd ever been able to maintain in the face of grand prix adversity.

Having kids was something he was going to have to think about as Caroline was becoming increasingly broody and he couldn't find it in his heart to deny her, however much he considered himself an unsuitable father. There was no reason why parenthood shouldn't be combined with some sort of management job in motor racing because whatever he'd said in an overwrought state at that damn silly press conference in Rio, the sport was his life.

It was in his blood, as it was in Caroline's to a different degree, and he had a nagging feeling that the next few months would show both of them that they couldn't live without it in some shape or form. Of one thing he was absolutely certain; he had taken the decision to quit of his own free will and he would never reproach Caroline over it.

For years with a wife he couldn't relate to, he hadn't really cared whether he lived or died and she had never given him an impression she bothered one way or the other. Some men filled that emotional desert, the empty quarter of their lives, with overwork, drink or drugs. With him it had been a matter of grappling with the more attractive groupies who made themselves available to take his mind off his problems.

He could see it all now, like a drunk recounting his life story at a session of Alcoholics Anonymous. He seemed to have been a sexaholic and the only cure was not going on the wagon, but finding a good woman. There had been no-one to make him feel a welcome addition to the human race. But the whole situation had changed and Caroline's love – a word that had always sat uneasily on his tongue – had been the catalyst. He had had his first taste of life with a loving woman, something millions took for granted with its logical outcome of children and domesticity.

Meanwhile, he had to cope with what was obviously going to be a horribly dreary, wet test session at Silverstone. Only Mercedes, he thought, would bother to re-invent the windscreen wiper as the big single blade with the cranked action shifted the pelting rain from the screen as he headed north up the A43.

God, how he hated rain in northern Europe. It always seemed wetter and colder than other parts of the world. You could get a heavy downpour in warmer climes and then the sun would come out and warm everything up in no time at all. If you were caught out in it, the sun would dry your clothes on you. Here, you'd get a cold in the head, if nothing worse.

As for racing open-wheeled single seaters in the wet it was madness, driving into a blinding ball of spray and just hoping for the best. It was more like Russian roulette than race driving. For once, everything had gone smoothly for him this season. Not only had there been the opportunity to drive for McColl, but every single race from Hockenheim onwards had been run in the dry. It had been a very lucky championship run.

Like all women who loved men with dangerous occupations, Caroline had wanted him to give up, but she'd been part of the sport long enough to know that no racing driver could be pressured into doing so. The decision had to come from him. You've made your bed, old bean, and now you've got to lie on it, he told himself. It was no use pretending; the doubts were setting in but at least he'd have the adorable Caroline to lie in the bed with him. What a contrast to the early days – when he and his wife had shared a bed – with Olivia's desiccated, sinewy frame, honed and hardened in contact with a hundred saddles. She had never wanted him yet she still made a fuss when he went elsewhere. Typical. But that was all over now.

Strange how life seemed to progress in eras; first the school years over which you had no control. They just happened to you. They had been followed by the false starts for which he was partly to blame; the year at Cambridge and the two in The Parachute Regiment. Then the 14 years in motor racing, resulting in his becoming the world champion. Who else was lucky enough to reach the top of this particular mountain with all his fingers and toes intact? He was now nearer 40 than 30 and an unknown future still beckoned. How many men could say that?

As he turned off the lane into the Silverstone main gate, the rain was still lashing down. The oilskinned and dripping young gateman beckoned him to stop instead of just waving him through.

"Sorry to hold you up, Mr Bastyan. I know I shouldn't really but I wonder, could I have your autograph?"

Alex took the young man's autograph book and the proffered pen. How contrary was the human spirit. When he'd been struggling all these years trying to get results with the wayward Tremayne, the autograph hunters had seemed nothing but an intrusion, a mockery. Why were they bothering him when he wasn't getting any results? Now that he had been able to achieve the championship there seemed some point in signing a kid's autograph book. But they wouldn't be asking him any more and he was going to miss it.

"What's your name?"

"Gary Smith, Mr Bastyan."

'To Gary, with best wishes, Alex Bastyan' he wrote neatly and returned the book.

"Gee, thanks," said the boy, grinning as though his cheeks would crack. "Good luck with the testing. Your team transporter got here half an hour ago."

" Thank you. I'm going to need it in weather like this," he said, waving goodbye to the young man who was still smiling as the rain ran down his face and dripped off the end of his nose.

Alex raised the window and drove towards the soggy infield, the pits and the paddock. A bedraggled Peter Foot was waiting to meet him at the door of the garage.

"Sorry about this, Alex. It's awful but we'll have to go ahead. The met people say it's not going to lift all day. I'll rustle up some coffee while you get your gear on. Dick's not here. He's already out in Japan. He always likes to combine races there with a few factory visits – you know Dick."

"How convenient for him, not having to put up with me, the great defector," said Alex with a mocking grin.

"Aw, c'mon Alex, it's not as bad as that. A lot of us here haven't given up on you, you know."

Alex shrugged. "Even if I changed my mind – which I'm not going to – Dick would never have me back."

"Peterboro McColl isn't quite the one-man band Dick sometimes thinks it is. Chuck Giordano controls the purse strings, not Dick, and he'd walk barefoot on hot coals to get you back."

"He would?"

"Told me himself. Somehow, I don't think you've got away from us as easily as you think. But enough of this gossiping. We've got some testing to do. There're some suspension and steering mods I want you to try. You remember you were saying at Rio that the turn-in wasn't as sharp as it should be. We've sorted out that brake problem you had at Jacarepagua so it should be all systems go for another nine points at Fuji. What a way to end the season!"

* * *

Alex wiped his driving boots on the little mat provided before standing on the seat and sliding down into the cockpit. The last thing he wanted was wet soles slipping on the pedals. Arms over his head, he wriggled his shoulders below the cockpit coaming, placed his hands on the tiny steering wheel and waited for the mechanic to strap him in.

The old unease at driving in the wet had set in like an Atlantic depression. At least there was only one other car lapping the circuit in a desultory sort of way.

"Mornin' Mr B!" said a once familiar voice over his right shoulder.

Alex was taken aback to find himself staring into the mocking eyes and broken-toothed grin of Terry Stevens.

"Smashin' day for driving in the rain and we all know 'ow much you like that, don't we, Mr B? I bet you didn't expect to see me again. That nice Mr Foot's taken me on temporary-like. I'm a sorta blast from the past."

More a rave from the grave, thought Alex, flicking his visor down slightly. He'd never got close enough to Stevens in the old Tremayne days to find out, but the man always gave the impression his breath could strip paint at ten paces.

"Nice to see you, Terry," he said unconvincingly. "Glad you've got fixed up again in Formula One."

"Well, you know what it's like in our game. Easy come, easy go." Leaning right over into the cockpit to give the crotch strap an excruciating heave that made Alex wince, he added with a look that was meant to be meaningful, "Some of us come and go a bit more easy than others."

Alex curtly nodded his thanks. Ridiculous though it was to be unsettled by seeing Stevens again, the man's sudden appearance had at least given him an incentive to get out on the circuit and get stuck in. He raised his right gloved hand, rotated his right index finger in the classic gesture for the starter to be plugged in and the engine fired up.

Nosing out from the garage he accelerated smoothly up the pit lane and on to the circuit. Pull yourself together man; there may be nobody in the stands but there's a world champion in the cockpit, he told himself. Avoiding the worst of the standing water where he could, Alex set about putting together some smooth laps at reduced speed. Silverstone had always been one of his favourite circuits and he was damned if he was going to let rain spoil his enjoyment of it completely. Smiling grimly to himself, he tried braking later before the corners and putting the power down earlier on those super straights. Ejecting rooster tails of spray from the grooved rain tyres, the McColl's lap times began to come down.

"What a hero," said Peter Foot clicking his stop watch. "I think he's done enough to give us some worthwhile feedback. We'll call him in next lap. This bloody rain is getting worse than ever. You can't drive in this."

* * *

This isn't test driving, Alex thought. It's a cross between submarine warfare and skating on extremely thin ice. And for what? He was world champion and he'd announced his retirement. What the hell was he doing it for? His dislike of driving in the wet was one of the sport's jokes yet here he was just showing off with no-one to watch anyway.

Was he trying to overcome his phobia? But this was cheating. It wasn't quite so bad when you had the track to yourself and didn't have to drive blind into a wall of spray. Driving in the wet was all about car control, calling for finesse in spades. He had even started to enjoy it in a masochistic sort of way, caressing the accelerator, being smoother than a politician's promises with his braking and changing of direction, until a niggling doubt began to surface.

Was he imagining it over the last two laps or was the steering becoming less predictable than even the frightful conditions warranted? He approached Becketts, that right-hander that leads into Chapel curve and the long Hangar straight. He feathered the brake pedal as he passed the trackside marker board, ideally positioned to turn in and clip the apex of the corner for the thirteenth time that morning.

He turned the wheel. There was no change of direction and the McColl ploughed straight on. He hit the brake pedal, not that it would do much good when there was so little contact with the track surface anyway. With no steering he couldn't hope to induce a spin, slow things down and reduce the impact with the bank. Shit!

This was going to be the biggest shunt he'd ever had. He was right – that lack of steering precision had turned – in an instant – to outright failure. McColls weren't supposed to break but this one had. In the middle of Beckett's. In the wet. The racing driver's ultimate nightmare of a mechanical disaster at speed was upon him.

This was no bad dream from which he would wake up sweating and try to dismiss with a curse, a shake of the head, a drink of water and return to sleep. It was Silverstone on one of the foulest days of the year and he was a passenger at his own accident, powerless to do anything about it. What a way to go. What a sodding stupid waste when he now had everything to live for ...

Young fighter pilots, crashing out of control in wartime dog fights, have been heard by stricken ground controllers crying out for their mothers over the aircraft's radio in the final seconds of life.

As the McColl ploughed through the catch-fencing and struck the earth bank head-on, brought to a complete stop from 100 mph in a distance of two feet, one word escaped Alex Bastyan. Screamed at the top of his voice in the muffled tumult of his battered helmet, it was: "CAROLINE!"

* * *

Peter Foot and his team had been listening to the clear-cut rise and fall in the engine note as the car had been lapping.

"For someone who's always made such a fuss about driving in the wet, Alex's not doing too –"

Suddenly there was a silence.

"My God! He's crashed!"

The rescue, fire truck and ambulance men were already at the scene by the time the McColl men had piled into their vehicles and raced across the old runway to the inside of Beckett's. Only Terry Stevens stayed behind.

Peter Foot and the McColl mechanics were aghast when they reached the spot. They had all seen badly damaged Formula One cars before but this one resembled nothing so much as a gigantic crumpled tube of toothpaste. It was a tangled, truncated wreck from nose to cockpit. And the world champion was still inside it.

Foot was suddenly aware that one of the crash crew was speaking to him. "What did you say?" he asked.

"How much fuel is there on board?" the man repeated irritably. Like anyone at the scene of a bad accident he was stressed and anxious to get an awful job done as soon as possible.

"Very little. We put in just enough for the testing. The tanks must be nearly empty."

"Thank God for that. Alex's got enough on his plate without dowsing everything with foam. We've got some cutting to do but this bloody deluge'll be on our side for once."

The crash crew cut, bent and spread the crumpled bodywork with the care and precision of brain surgeons for 20 minutes before it was possible to ease Alex like a blood-soaked lifeless marionette from the wreckage and place him on a stretcher on the ground.

"Will he live?" asked an ashen Peter Foot.

"Only God knows that," said an ambulanceman, grimly.

One of the young mechanics turned aside to be sick as the unrelenting rain beat down.

"It's one of the worst impacts I've ever seen, coming to a dead stop in such a short distance," said the man from the rescue truck. "If it hadn't been one of your cars, Peter, we'd be pulling out a corpse."

"What are his injuries?"

"Can't tell till they examine him in Northampton General," said the ambulance man, giving mouth to mouth resuscitation and compressing Alex's chest. "He's got no pulse I can find and he's losing blood fast. At a guess I'd say left leg broken in half a dozen places at least, right leg ditto if not more. His pelvis is bound to be shattered because of the shock being transmitted through the legs and there'll be hip joints broken and ribs gone. Are you coming in the ambulance?"

"Of course," said Foot.

Siren wailing, lights flashing, the ambulance set off on its 14 mile dash up the A43, via Towcester, to Northampton General Hospital. As gatekeeper Gary Smith watched it go, the rain running down his face was augmented by tears.

25

The telephone shrilled on Detective Superintendent Brian Kinsman's desk. How he wished they could quieten the things down a bit. He might be the oldest person in the building but he wasn't deaf yet.

Kinsman was one of the few men in the force who'd actually done National Service. As befitted his six foot four inches he had served two years in the Irish Guards and disappointed his company commander, who wanted him to sign on as a regular. A glittering career was dangled in front of him but life in married quarters with constant moves as the battalion was posted did not appeal to a man who valued his home life above anything.

Besides, he had an uncle in the police who had persuaded him that keeping law and order was of more practical use than being a mere cog in the machine of world peace. The Brigade of Guards had their place but the American nuclear deterrent had the major role. The argument had not been lost on the logically minded young Kinsman and on returning home to Northampton he had joined the force.

For over 20 years he had been commuting from Paulersbury to the art deco 1930s Odeon-Gothic style building in Campbell Square. He had the misfortune to be born too soon in the days when skill in Latin was required before anybody was deemed suitable for higher education. By temperament he was a studious, thoughtful, painstaking man who would have made an excellent schoolmaster or lecturer at a redbrick university – in anything but Latin.

Instead however he spent his working life doing his utmost to bring law-breakers to justice. Criminals were nasty, untidy little men with no respect for the norms of society, and the sooner the semiliterate, bejeaned and leather jacketed young thugs who comprised most of his workload were behind bars, the better.

They had no conception of the shock and outrage felt by people who had had their homes broken into, their valuables stolen, drawers and cupboards ransacked, often their carpets fouled with human excrement by these wasters who put on such a pathetic air once they were caught. If he could have his way no-one would sit in judgement who hadn't personally been on the receiving end of this rising tide of housebreaking and burglary.

Was it any wonder vigilante groups of householders were springing up all over Britain to protect themselves from these vicious young men whose sole aim in life was to feed a drug habit and avoid doing a stroke of honest work. Privately he had every sympathy with the good citizens, officially he had to toe the line and say that law and order was solely the job of the police. How could it be? They couldn't be everywhere. With the growing drug culture imported from America which nobody seemed able to contain, the problem could only get worse. He was not sorry to be retiring later in the year and wished his successor well in his thankless task.

"Kinsman here," he said into the phone.

"I'm sorry to trouble you ..."

It was a woman's voice, soft, well modulated, essentially

officer's wife. Twenty-five years ago if he'd been in the orderly room and heard it he would've found himself almost sitting to attention and saying 'Mam'. He wondered if things were still the same but doubted it. They never were these days.

"How may I help you, madam?" he enquired courteously, wondering why the call had come unfiltered directly through to his extension.

"My name won't mean anything to you. It's Caroline Tremayne and I'm ringing from Tokyo ..."

"Yes?"

The woman seemed strangely hesitant. But she obviously wasn't one of those nutters wasting police time. She'd tell him what she had to in due course. Over many years of police work he'd learned that patience wasn't only a virtue. It was a necessity.

"I wonder if you've seen the headlines?"

Like many senior policemen, Kinsman took The Daily Telegraph which he didn't have time to read till he got home in the evenings and wrestled with the crossword. He couldn't remember anything which might have any particular relevance to a call from a well-spoken woman ringing from Japan.

"Perhaps it's on the sports pages but I'd have thought most papers would have it on the front page," she said.

Kinsman was now intrigued. What could this piece of news be that this woman with the charming voice was so hesitant in bringing to his attention? It must be important to her or she wouldn't be calling from all that distance where it was probably the middle of the night or something weird.

"According to an English language newspaper I've just seen, the headline is CHAMPION FIGHTS FOR LIFE AFTER CRASH and everybody here is full of it. The Japanese Grand Prix is on at Fuji this weekend. But I'm dropping everything and getting the first plane I can back to Heathrow. Then I'll go straight to Northampton General."

So there was a local connection. At least they seemed to be getting somewhere. The woman at times seemed to be having difficulty keeping her emotions under control but presumably they'd get to the bottom of it soon.

"Don't you think you'd better start at the beginning, Mrs Tremayne, and tell me all about it?"

"Yes. Thank you for being so patient with me. I wish I wasn't so far away on the other side of the world and then I might have more accurate information myself. Basically it's this. Alex Bastyan, the new world champion – he was only confirmed as the champion after the Brazilian Grand Prix 10 days ago – was testing at Silverstone. I understand it was a last minute affair before the team and the cars were air-freighted out here. But he had a terrible accident and was rushed to Northampton General ..."

Of course. Kinsman remembered having seen something about it on the Central Television news, having missed the main national newscast. When it came to reading The Telegraph's sports coverage he confined himself to the cricket news and the fortunes of his beloved Northamptonshire. They excelled at the one-day game, having won the Gilette in 1976 and the Benson and Hedges in 1980, but little else these days.

He had registered the news of the crash at Silverstone with the normal sympathy that anyone feels for a fellow human who has been badly injured. Sadly, motor racing accidents were by no means uncommon. It had not meant a great deal to him and still less could he now understand why it could be a police matter and the subject of a long-distance call from Tokyo. However, it was something he would discuss that evening with his son, Peter, who was a complete and utter motor racing enthusiast.

"I'm sorry, madam. I do recall seeing something about it now. But how does that concern us in Northampton Police?"

"I don't know how to put this, superintendent, but I'm not at all sure that it was ... an accident. You see, I'm afraid Alex was the sort of man who tended to make enemies. I've a feeling his car might have been sabotaged."

It was out in the open now. But it all seemed a bit far-fetched. Perhaps she was a nutter after all, although she didn't sound like one. They invariably had a strange timbre to their voices and Mrs Tremayne sounded quite normal. It was time to try to find out a bit more.

"May I ask what your connection with all this is? We've had no information on similar lines from any other source."

"Alex Bastyan and I hope to be married," she said.

"I see," he replied hesitantly. "What exactly are your grounds for supposing that anyone might want to injure your ... fiancé?"

"He's not exactly my fiancé. We're both married but we had hoped to divorce and be together as soon as possible. And now this has happened –" Kinsman thought he heard a stifled sob at the other end and waited a few seconds for Mrs Tremayne to compose herself. "I have no specific grounds but as I said just now, I'm afraid Alex trod on a lot of toes. He's a controversial man – always has been. There's a lot of people around who wish him harm."

Anybody else would've been sent packing ages ago but Kinsman, ever the gentleman, felt obliged to help this lady – she was hardly a maiden – in distress.

"You must understand, madam, that this only becomes a police matter if it can be proved that the wrecked car has been tampered with. That may take a long time to prove. If it *is* proved then we have to try to find the person or persons who might've had a sufficient grudge against him – and the opportunity, don't forget – to sabotage his car. All I can suggest at this time is that you get in touch with us as soon as you get back to Britain. I'll get one of my men to get a statement from you and we'll take it from there. I'm afraid that's the best I can do right now. Meanwhile I'll make some enquiries at this end."

"Thank you, superintendent. You've been most kind. Goodbye."

"Not at all, we'll wait to hear from you." As soon as he had put the phone down, he called Detective Constable Kevin

Owens from the CID general office just down the corridor.

"Pop in and see me for a moment, will you, constable?"

As became an ex-Guardsman, Kinsman ran a disciplined office. Unless on undercover assignments, detectives were expected to dress neatly and wear collar and tie and have their hair cut to a reasonable length.

"You're policemen, not window cleaners," he would frequently remind his officers. "I expect the great British public to be able to tell my men from the villains. There will be no jeans and trainers in this squad."

Similarly, the gradations of rank were strictly observed and he was called Sir. The only exception to this iron rule was DC Owens who was allowed the role of court jester. However indulgent Kinsman was with him, he couldn't stomach the use of guv. Owens, however, was permitted to call him boss.

"What do you know about motor racing, constable?" he asked when the portly Owens made his appearance. For a young man he looked remarkably overweight. Too much beer and junk food, Kinsman always thought.

"Zilch, boss," said Owens. "I'm a Man United fan."

"So you won't have heard about the new world champion's crash at Silverstone the other day and you're not aware that he is, as we speak, fighting for his life in Northampton General?"

"I knew *that*, boss, but what's that got to do with us?"

"Would you be surprised to know that I've just had a call from Tokyo from a lady who thinks his car may have been sabotaged?"

"I'd be gobsmacked, boss."

"I was a bit surprised myself to get this call ..." Kinsman checked his blotter because his memory wasn't as good as it used to be, " ... from a Mrs Caroline Tremayne."

"She rang, did she?"

"You know this lady?"

"I know *of* her. She's the wife of Freddie Tremayne, the guy who runs the Tremayne team. You see her picture in the gossip columns now and again, mainly I think because she's such a cracker."

"You're very well informed, constable," said Kinsman, a trifle miffed. "I thought you said you didn't know anything about motor racing."

"I don't, boss. Not in the same sense as being able to tell you who won the French Grand Prix in 1960 and which years Fangio was world champion. But of course I've heard of Alex Bastyan. He's the first world champion Britain's had for years and it's a cryin' shame that he's had this shunt within a few days of announcing his retirement. Some of the tabloids say that he only packed it in so he could be with Caroline Tremayne."

"Interesting," mused Kinsman. "She's just told me they hoped to be married after they'd got their respective divorces. Perhaps there are some people around who would like to prevent that happy event ... Here's what I want you to do. She's flying back from Tokyo to the bedside and has promised to get in touch. As soon as we hear from her I want you to get her statement."

"But all the Formula One folk are out in Japan now, boss. That's where I ought to be," said Owens, tongue in cheek.

Kinsman couldn't resist a smile. One of things he liked about Owens was his sense of humour. Besides, he wasn't a bad detective and if only he's learn to take more care of his appearance and smarten himself up, he might go far. "There's no question of that and you know it. Can you imagine my accounting to the Police Committee for air fares and hotel bills in ruddy Japan? I don't know a great deal about motor racing either but I know a young man who does. I'll pick his brains when I get home."

"You mean young Peter?"

"Who else? Not only is his bedroom wall plastered with posters of racing cars – he also spends all his money on the magazines. Still, it's a healthier interest than these ghastly so-called rock stars."

"Don't knock the rock, boss," said Owens with a grin.

"Knock it? I'd like to kick it into touch for good and all!"

* * *

Kinsman was surprised at his son's concern and depth of feeling over Alex Bastyan's accident when they discussed the matter at the supper table that night.

"I'm chairman of his fan club at school, Dad," Peter pointed out. "It's not official, of course, and we don't write to him and ask for autographs or anything silly like that. It's just a group of us in the sixth form who're keen on motor sport and follow Formula One closely. Richard Elliott was saying at school today that his dad reckons that, OK, Alex is a press-on driver but no-one who's just announced his retirement and hates driving in the wet is going to stick his neck out in a grotty test session at Silverstone. He's quite convinced something must've broken. And don't forget McColls are famous for *not* breaking."

"That's interesting," mused Kinsman. "Perhaps there's something in the conspiracy theory after all ..."

"What'll you do about it, Dad, or can't you tell me?"

"There's not a lot we can do unless the accident investigation shows evidence of sabotage. Still, I've arranged to get a statement from Mrs Tremayne when she's back from Japan."

"What's she coming to Northampton for, Dad? Alex left the Tremayne team after the French Grand Prix in July."

"To be by the bedside, of course."

Peter looked puzzled. "That's nice of her."

"I'm sure she's a very pleasant and caring person," said Kinsman with a smile.

* * * * *

"A good piece of work, constable," said Kinsman, tapping the slim buff folder on his desk with the stem of his pipe.

"Thank you, boss," said Owens. "I had a ton of co-operation not only from Mrs Tremayne but she put me on to a journalist who was a mine of information – I had a long session with him on the phone. What that man Morgan don't know about motor racing and the people in it ain't worth knowing."

"Good," murmured Kinsman. "That's what I like to hear, No-one could accuse us of wasting the rate-payers' money with expensive enquiries. Now let's see who would either benefit from having Alex Bastyan out of the way or who hated him so much they would cheerfully try to put him out of action.

"First on my list would be this chap Tremayne who's not only lost his wife to the man but also had his racing team's prospects seriously damaged by Bastyan's defection. From your enquiries, constable, what do you think of that as a proposition?"

"I agree on the face of it, Freddie Tremayne could be a major suspect but it don't stand up, I'm afraid, when you know something about the man. He couldn't hurt a fly and everybody says he's one of the good guys in Formula One. Too nice. That's probably why he and his team haven't done better – he simply ain't got enough of the killer instinct for the sport, let alone actually killing another human being."

"It's not unknown for the mildest of men to snap and murder the men who've run off with their wives," Kinsman pointed out.

"Not this one, boss. Besides, even if he wanted to, how could he stick a spanner on the works of a rival team's car?"

"Never heard of the hired hit man, constable? You don't do the job yourself, you pay someone else. Couldn't he've bribed a McColl mechanic? I'm only playing devil's advocate here, you understand."

"No way, boss. Not only his own wife, but this Welsh guy Morgan says he's convinced that Tremayne couldn't have done anything like that."

"All right, then, We'll cross him off the list. What about Mrs Bastyan? What's her name, Olivia? Was it a love match? Was she devastated by Bastyan leaving her for Mrs Tremayne?"

"Again, no way. I bet she was probably glad to have got rid of him. There's no suggestion it was much of a love match. For years before he and Mrs Tremayne started their relationship, Bastyan was reputed to have a girl at every circuit. They both lived their own lives and did their own thing.

"Him with Formula One and his women and her with her show jumping. There's no suggestion that there were other males in her life. The only ones there were had four hooves, long tails and manes. It was no love match and the received wisdom is, boss, that Bastyan married her for her father's money in the first place. They finally split up in September, not long after he went to the McColl team."

Kinsman, who had never needed any woman apart from Doreen, his wife for 25 years, listened to the description of Bastyan's marriage with some distaste. "Two down and two to go. Next on the list is the team-mate Thibault, the Frenchman. He had no reason to love Bastyan, by all accounts."

"Bad blood between Formula One team-mates is par for the course," said Owens, "but it doesn't lead to attempted murder. The animosity isn't life-long because they all move around so much. Next year there's someone else to hate, don't forget. Bastyan had left the Tremayne team by the end of July so whatever he'd done to upset Thibault would've been water under the bridge by now. Mixin' my metaphors a bit but I hope you get my meaning, boss."

Ever the stickler, Kinsman despaired of correct English

from Owens in conversation but insisted on it in written reports. The man could express himself perfectly well but, like his generation, he tended towards the slovenly in the spoken word. They all spent too much time watching American films and the crime shows on television where the criminal was miraculously apprehended in time for the nine o'clock news, and the detectives were barely distinguishable from the criminals in appearance and behaviour. But credit where it was due, Owens had done a workmanlike job and obviously knew more about motor racing than he was prepared to let on in his odd self-denigratory way.

"Right, constable. So that leaves – according to your excellent report – just the mechanic. Stevens isn't it?"

"He's our man, boss. No doubt about it. He's got motive, opportunity, the complete works. He's such a nutcase though he'd get away with diminished responsibility, unfit to plead and all them other get-outs the nutters use. He was even heard sayin' that Bastyan had seduced his 16-year-old daughter as well as gettin' him the sack. He'd convinced himself he had every reason for wantin' a lot of harm to come to the man."

"Why bother?" asked Kinsman drily. "I would've thought there was an excellent chance that a driver is going to be badly hurt – or even killed – in the normal course of events."

"You're right there, boss. There ain't many who've gone through an entire career without gettin' seriously injured. But even when they are, they're back in the cockpit before you can say grand prix. They recuperate 10 times quicker than the average patient. They just can't wait to get back and do it again. Barmy I call it. The day I get so much as a nose bleed caused by some villain I'm resignin' and findin' another line of work. I rather fancy flower arrangin' you know, boss."

"Thank you for letting me know, constable. Don't forget roses can draw blood too. To be serious, you're convinced Stevens wasn't prepared to leave it to chance and took it upon himself to expedite matters by arranging for Bastyan's car to suffer some failure?"

"Sure of it, boss. Though how you prove it I dunno. We'd need a witness who actually saw him tampering with whatever it was. Ironic, innit, if it turns out Bastyan gets his comeuppance over the one female he never touched. There's no evidence that he ever met Stevens' daughter, let alone screwed her."

"Your report stays on file and we'll just have to wait and see what the technical examination of the wrecked car turns up. If the experts can prove to my satisfaction that the car was tampered with, we'll pull Stevens in for questioning. Unless or until that happens our hands are tied, constable."

"So that's it. A waiting game, eh, boss? Alex Bastyan may've made enemies in the sport. But there's no denyin' his popularity with the public. You should see the flowers, cards and letters that've been floodin' into the hospital."

"I don't see why we should be surprised," said Kinsman. "He's just become world champion and announced his retirement. Then he suffers this terrible accident. There'll be a lot of public sympathy over that. I've been learning quite a bit about him. Young Peter tells me he's been Britain's best racing driver for a few seasons now. He's got all the books on the sport and wonders why we don't rate our motor racing stars as highly as we used to. In the 1930s the speed kings like Malcolm Campbell, Segrave and company were knighted. Nowadays even a world champion is lucky to get an OBE."

"What about Jack Brabham? He was knighted after he'd packed it in."

"I think you'll find - according to my informant – that he was honoured in the Australian list which still means that no English or Scottish world champion has been kighted by our Government. Young Peter gets incandescent pointing to the footballers, cricketers and jockeys who get knighted while world champion racing drivers only get what he calls 'measly OBEs.

"You know, I think the boy's right," Kinsman went on thoughtfully. "For men who risk their necks in extreme sports an OBE isn't enough. They're bringing great prestige to their country and yet all the recognition they get is the gong given automatically to a time-serving civil servant who's done nothing more adventurous than shuffle a mountain of paper for twenty years. The certainty of the bauble is also seen as a way of keeping civil servants loyal and preventing them from quitting and earning more in industry – as if most of them could!

"A very useful tool is the honours system. The possibility of OBEs, CBEs and even knighthoods dangled over the heads of back bench MPs has kept many a government in power far longer than it deserved. It's the same with the trade unions and pressure groups that can cause a bit of trouble for the ruling party. All of them know it – that the gong that goes with the job won't be forthcoming and the general secretary, director-general, or whoever it may be, won't feature in the New Year or Birthday honours if he's been too critical of government policy. Given the value that people attach to something that purports to come from the Queen herself – God bless her – it takes a very principled individual to say what needs to be said and to hell with the gong."

Owens listened to his chief with growing disbelief.

"This is fightin' talk from you, boss," he said. "I always thought you was establishment through and through."

Kinsman smiled. "That's what you've all been meant to think for years. I'm a closet rebel and vote Liberal. Now that I'm coming up for retirement I can say what I like. I've always felt that an honours system should be that – a reward for genuine achievement – not a means of keeping lick-spittles and time-servers in line. There should be a difference between genuinely deserved honours and gongs for the boys."

"There is," said Owens. "There's the OBN, Order of the Brown Nose."

"But that's not official." Kinsman laughed. "Even the civil servants refer to the OBE as Other Buggers' Efforts and the MBE as My Bloody Efforts. The CMG is Call me God and

KCMG is Kindly Call me God. No, to a kid like mine world champions are gods and I think they deserve far more of their country than a middle ranking civil servant's OBE when it comes to honours."

"Couldn't agree more, boss. I'd need a bloomin' VC to get into one of them F1 cars, let alone try to drive it in anger. Everyone of them drivers is a bleedin' hero as far as I'm concerned.

"But you know, boss, the fans can't understand why Alex Bastyan packed it in. That Welsh journalist guy Morgan reckons it really is because of Caroline Tremayne. For the first time in his life he's found something – someone – who means more to him than motor racing. He's achieved what he set out to do: become World Champion at the ripe old age of 36 so now's the time to call it a day and spend time with his woman. You should see her, boss. Even after sitting up all night on the red-eye from Tokyo, she could still get an undertaker's convention dancing the tango. She's that sexy – but in a ladylike way. I couldn't take my eyes off of her. Cor!"

Kinsman cleared his throat, loudly disapproving. Like many repressed men with iron self-control, he found the idea of any sexual freedom disturbing. "You forget I've spoken to Mrs Tremayne who sounds every inch a lady – whatever her extra-marital relationships may be. You're always on about her. Tell me something about the wife, constable. How does she strike you?"

"What can I say, boss? These sports stars' women are in a different league. Look at all them footballers' wives. Everyone of them drop-dead gorgeous. Mrs B is just a bit too skinny for my taste, too horsey. She looks as though she'd smell of mash and saddle soap if you get my meanin'. It's all a matter of 'orses for courses, ain't it, boss? It all depends on whether your taste runs more to Twiggy than Sophia Loren, I suppose. I certainly wouldn't put a bag over 'er head – as the sayin' goes. She's no Doris Karloff, that's for sure."

Kinsman suppressed a smile. It was useless to expect any

worthwhile character assessments from Owens where women were concerned. To the detective, anyone in a skirt who wasn't plug-ugly could only be a sex object.

"You're exactly what my newly liberated wife would call a male chauvinist pig," said Kinsman with a mock exasperation. "Has it ever crossed your mind that when it comes to answering maidens' prayers you would only be acceptable where avoirdupois is deemed an asset? I suggest a transfer to the Tonga Constabulary."

"Who cares, boss? That's the great thing about being a bloke. There's no way I fancy being a bird, and with my luck, can you see me 'avin great boobs an' legs and a phizog to match? It don't matter what we look like 'cos we pull them with our brains, not our looks. And – thank God – they're daft enough to fall for the corniest of chat-up lines. Look at the cases we've had where women you'd think would have had more sense give their life savings to a con artist. It's just as well for the fair sex I only use my talents to con them out of their knickers and not their dosh. Kev Silver Tongue they call me."

"Not in the witness box, they don't."

"Perhaps not, boss."

One look at his chief's unsmiling face told Owens it was time to cool it and get real again.

"It's bloody tragic," he went on, "after all those years and all those crashes Bastyan walked away from – that this should happen. And just when he's announced his retirement. I wouldn't know meself but experts like Morgan say he was never a natural but had to work very hard at it. He started much later than most grand prix drivers and had no background in the sport. Many come from some sort of motor sport tradition with fathers who used to race a bit and took them along to the tracks when they was young, or had dads in the motor trade - something like that. Alex Bastyan didn't. I never realised that."

"I don't suppose many people do," mused Kinsman. Where sport was concerned, he was interested only in cricket. When he was a boy the top racing drivers had been called speed kings and their dominions were the race tracks of the world. Bastyan's kingdom was now a bed in intensive care at Northampton General. It had been a mighty fall.

"I suppose we all tend to take our sportsmen and public figures for granted," he went on. "Who knows whether the Boy Botham learned his cricket skills in the back garden or whether the Prime Minister acquired her taste for politics at Alderman Roberts's knee?" He paused for a moment and then continued, as if thinking aloud: "From what you say, marriage to the millionaire's daughter can't've made the young Bastyan many friends in his early days."

"Sure boss, but other drivers soon realised that this was no rich-kid-by-proxy playing at it. When he kept crashing because he was trying too hard, his father-in-law's money gave him an edge because he could afford new cars and repairs that would've bankrupted most of his rivals. To that extent he did have an advantage but he learned the hard way all right.

"Morgan told me that Bastyan was always the perfect gent, never braggin' about all the dosh he could get hold of. He would always help out another driver in the paddock if he could. But it was different in the race where it was a case of no holds barred. He was a terrorist on the Tarmac but a good mate off of it. The other drivers soon learned to keep out of his way and they knew he'd get to the very top – or kill 'isself. Since he's been a world figure in the sport his fan club's grown by leaps and bloomin' bounds. He got a load of brownie points for stickin' it out with Tremayne all those years when it was obvious the team was over the hill. That's what they call Quixotic innit, boss?"

Kinsman nodded. "A rare attribute among highly paid sportsmen," he remarked wryly. "I must say I'm quite impressed by your background knowledge, constable."

"Thanks, boss. It's all stuff I got from my informant. He told me nobody blamed Bastyan for switching teams in mid-season. Half the grand prix field would've jumped at the chance if they could've broken their contracts. Everybody admired the way he kept his nerve, drove brilliantly and won the title in a car he'd only had for half a season. Morgan told me he reckoned it would go down as one of motor racing's real great achievements.

"You know what else he told me, boss? He said the fans like Alex Bastyan because he's a racer and doesn't give a damn. They know he'll always drive balls-out – as they put it – and not pussy-foot about driving a canny race to pick up a few points. They know he'll always go for broke.

"Kids love him because he's got this reputation for being a good bad guy – doing all the things they'd like to do but get told off for. And he got to do it in a racing car! He's every kid's hero. Men like him because he's a man's man. Women love him because they know he loves them."

Kinsman tapped out his pipe in the ashtray on his desk. "Ah yes, the women..." he murmured wistfully. "Caroline Tremayne and the wife – we mustn't forget her – keeping the vigil .... the women in his life. It's probably just as well they haven't all turned up."

"Why's that, boss?"

There could almost have been an element of envy in Kinsman's reply: "From what you've told me constable, uniform branch couldn't spare the men to control the queues round the block and prevent catfights in the car park."

"It's not only all the women he's had," said Owens. "There's oodles of fans out there *willing* him to recover. And make a comeback."

DRIVERS WORLD CHAMPIONSHIP	SAFRICA	LONG BEACH	MONACO	SAN MARINO	BELGIUM	BRITAIN	FRANCE	GERMANY	SPAIN	HOLLAND	AUSTRIA	ITALY	CANADA	BRAZIL	JAPAN	TOTAL
GIANNI ABATI (Ita) *McColl-Renault*	9	9		6		4										**28**
ERWIN SCHRAMMER (WGer) *McColl-Renault*			6								1	2				**9**
JUAN BALTIERI (Arg) *Brabham-Ford*		4			4		9			4	6			6		**33**
WIM HEEMSKERK (NL) *Brabham-Ford*		2							1				3		1	**7**
GUY ANTONIAZZI (Ita) *Ferrari V-12*	4			9			4	6					6		9	**38**
DINO MORANDINI (Ita) *Ferrari V-12*	3				9		3		4			4				**23**
ALEX BASTYAN (GB) *Tremayne-Ford (also McColl-Renault)*			9					9	9	6	9	9	9	4		**64**
T-N THIBAULT (Fra) *Tremayne-Ford*	1	1					2			1				3	2	**10**
HUGO FALCUS (Bel) *Tyrrell-Ford*	6			3	3			2		3	4		4		6	**31**
GAVIN BROWN (GB) *Tyrrell-Ford*				2		3						3			3	**11**
HECTOR BONFANTE (Bra) *McLaren-Ford*		6		4		6	6	3	6	9				9		**49**
BENGT CHRISTENSEN (Swe) *McLaren-Ford*			4		2				3					1		**10**
ALAN MASON (GB) *Lotus-Ford*	2		3		6	9		4		2		6		2	4	**38**
PEDRO JALAPENO (Bra) *Lotus-Ford*		3				2		1	2		3	1	1			**13**
HARALD KASTNER (WGer) *Fantino-Mostyn*				1							2		2			**5**
TOSHIRO WATANABE (Jpn) *Fantino-Mostyn*						1										**1**
PATRICK BELLAMOUR (Fra) *Mistral-Ford*							1									**1**
ROLAND JONCHERY (Fra) *Mistral-Ford*				1												**1**